GEM'S STORY

I think Gem's story is a work of art. It's a blend of psychology, philosophy and spirituality combined with a wonderful talent of writing. Such a sensitivity! I enjoyed it as much as I learned from it.
Cimen Keskin, Istanbul, Turkey

In this day and age of action, violence and sex in fiction and video, it's a blessed relief to read something that restores and inspires; that speaks to the soul. Gem's Story is a timeless fable, a gentle lesson in finding God, and, yes, a love story—but not the usual sort of love story.
What the two main characters share is very special and rare, but the author imparts the hopeful message that we are all capable of this kind of spiritual love.
Francesca H. Kelly, USA, Former Editor-in-Chief of the web magazine *Tales from a Small Planet;*http://www.talesmag.com

I enjoyed 'Gem' very much and recommend it to anyone interested in spirituality and the spiritual path.
Acarya Viveka, Ananda Seva Mission

This book is a delight. Written in almost a hypnotic lyricism it tells the story of finding meaning on the path of life. I find it difficult to express the joy that I had in reading it. I have a hope, indeed a feeling that Gem's Story will become a classic, revered and enjoyed by young and old.
Dawn Akyürek, UK, Teacher of English Literature

I'm a great admirer of Gem and have a lot of respect for her wisdom.
I resort to this book every time I need some peace of mind, or need to commune with people I really care about, at times of inner unrest.
I can't come up with any adjective good enough to describe the benefit and positive influence that Gem's Story can bring into one's life.
Renuka Ramesh, India

Gem's Story
- A Spiritual Journey

Two people search for the purpose of Life.
They find more than they expect...

Gem's Story
- A Spiritual Journey

Two people search for the purpose of Life.
They find more than they expect...

Joost Boekhoven

COSMIC
EGG
BOOKS

Winchester, UK
Washington, USA

First published by Cosmic Egg Books, 2013
Cosmic Egg Books is an imprint of John Hunt Publishing Ltd., Laurel House, Station Approach,
Alresford, Hants, SO24 9JH, UK
office1@jhpbooks.net
www.johnhuntpublishing.com

For distributor details and how to order please visit the 'Ordering' section on our website.

Text copyright: Joost Boekhoven 2012

ISBN: 978 1 78099 876 3

A CIP catalogue record for this book is available from the British Library.

Design: Lee Nash

Printed in the USA by Edwards Brothers Malloy

We operate a distinctive and ethical publishing philosophy in all
areas of our business, from our global network of authors to
production and worldwide distribution.

CONTENTS

– Gem, you call your spiritual teacher "Master". What is a Master?
– A master is someone who has mastered an art. A chess master has mastered the art of playing chess. A spiritual Master is someone who has mastered the art of living.

– Can I become a spiritual Master?
– You can—when you love yourself enough.

(from Ask Gem: *personal answers to spiritual questions)*

Prologue

Autumn, Second Moon

One of the birds that fly in big, lazy circles above our village must have seen him coming. In the beginning, he was only a speck in the endless plains. Later, the speck became a tiny figure. Still later, the speck grew into a man, a sturdy man walking steadily towards our village. He took slow, imperturbable steps as if nothing in the world could shake him.

The same bird might have seen me as well, a dark-haired girl sitting high in the tamarind tree near the center of the village. The late-afternoon sun felt warm on my skin, but I hardly noticed it. I had pulled up my legs until my knees touched my chin, and hugged them tightly. I was thinking.

I didn't see the man coming. I didn't know who he was.

I had no idea what would happen.

The Visitor

Where do we come from?
Why are we here?
Where are we going?
- Gem

Autumn, Second Moon, two-hands' day

The dogs are usually the first to let us know. From my secluded place high in the tamarind tree, I could see them running to the market place today, barking and yelping to alarm us, and then running back again. Chickens scurried away to all sides; geese honked indignantly. In the light of the setting sun, pigs looked up from their digging in the mud between the huts and grunted their disapproval. Children joined in the confusion and ran in a cloud of dust towards the place the dogs came from, the western entrance of the village. It was like the times when my father and I entered a new village, with our ox-cart full of merchandise.

Finally, I saw the cause of all the commotion. It was one single man, tall, strongly built, walking barefoot and wearing a worn-out brown mantle. On his back, he carried a small bag. His beard was wild, and his head bald, except for a ring of very short brown hair. He walked slowly, with dignity, his tall frame straight. With the setting sun behind him, he threw a long shadow on the road.

His face showed he was fortyish, some twenty harvests older than I am. But his way of walking made me think of a wise old man. Somebody who had seen much, thought much, and understood much.

From my high viewpoint, I saw him walk down the

street. From behind trees, children watched him; hidden in their houses, the adults looked at him. Nobody came outside.

I think I watched more intently than anybody else. He seemed somebody special. I felt a strange kind of peace looking at him. After a while, I got the feeling that I wanted to talk to him.

That made me quite uncomfortable. I hardly ever come out of the tree. I only do it to help with the harvests, or when there is a fire. My uncle gave me a hut near the river, but most of the year I stay in my tree hut. From that place, I can see much of what is happening in the village and nobody disturbs me. I have peace, and I can think about why we are living, where we come from and why people are as they are.

I like people—from a distance. Whenever I come down from the tree, somebody tells me it is long time I got married. There are enough women in the village, but people tell me about Ast, how strong he is, and Hari, how gentle he is, and about Vrek and At and what's his name...

It scares me like anything. Imagine being in a hut with a strange man. Never.

So I stay in the tree most of the time. But now I saw the stranger reach the market place. He looked around. I saw him come to a decision.

He walked towards Bom's house—and I knew he was walking straight into trouble.

Autumn, Second Moon, tenth day

I had been traveling for several days in this region and the languages seemed to differ considerably from village to village. I found it more and more difficult to make myself understood. An extra obstacle was that the concept of monk, a wanderer devoted to God who needs a bit of bread and a place for the night, seemed to be unknown in these places.

When I entered Pir this afternoon—I learned the village's name only later today—I was tired and hungry. I saw people looking at me from a distance, hiding in their houses. Even the children didn't come to me. Slowly I walked to what seemed to be the central place and let God guide me to a house.

At the opening of the hut, I called *hello* in the language of the previous village, hoping it would work here, and when I heard a grunt from inside I stepped in.

I found myself in a dark, smoky room. Two men and an old woman were sitting by a fireplace. I said the local equivalent of *hello* again, and was met by a suspicious silence. I tried a few other words that might be appropriate.

The silence continued.

The old woman finally muttered one word to the younger of the two men. He nodded slowly and stood up, his eyes on me. He reached for a long stained knife, which hung over the fireplace.

Local customs differ widely in this area, but I was fairly sure this was not part of a welcoming ceremony. I turned around and left the hut.

Just outside I stood still. The square was still empty, but I felt many eyes on me again. I looked around. Nobody showed himself. From behind me, in the hut, I heard slow footsteps coming. What did God want me to do here, I wondered?

At that instant, rapid light feet came down the street towards me. The next moment a young girl stood in front of me. I estimated her to be thirteen, fourteen maybe. She looked very serious.

Involuntarily I held my breath. She had beautiful long black hair, outlined by the setting sun behind her; her face was finely cut and had a touch of far away eastern countries. She differed from all other women I had seen in this area.

I always avoided women here. They were crude and had no sense of decency. But this girl was different. I saw now that she must be older than I guessed, maybe even twenty. Her subtleness had made me think she was so young.

She looked at the ground when she spoke to me. I didn't understand her words, but I was struck by her voice. She sounded so humble.

She sounded *apologetic*. For what? For the behavior of her fellow-villagers here? No. I suddenly understood. She was apologizing for the fact that she talked to me.

I did something I never did to women. I smiled at her.

What struck me most was his dignity, and the gentleness in his face. There was no trace of crudeness. The gentleness even made up for his unkempt beard that gave him, at first sight, a wild appearance. With such a beard, he looked like one of the *meandi*, the madmen that roamed the plains around our village. Parents used to threaten misbehaving children that the *meandi* would come and take them away.

But this man was very different. I couldn't believe nobody else saw it.

I knew that everyone was looking at me when I went to him. I felt so embarrassed. I never talked in public. I never talked to men I had not been introduced to. But he needed help. Bom stood behind him in the entrance of his hut, stroking his knife. Nobody would do anything if he killed the man.

"Maybe I can be of help..." I said to the stranger, softly, looking at the ground, trying to find words that fitted with his dignity. Suddenly the thought struck me that he might not want to talk to me, a mere girl.

But he smiled. His smile sent a wave of warmth through me. I almost lost my balance. This was not Ast's possessive grin, or Hari's anxious smile. It was a warm, giving smile. It reminded me painfully of my father. No one else had acted like this towards me before. I felt I could trust this stranger.

At the same time, that feeling was so scary, I wanted

to run away and hide in my tree. It was only with an effort I could stay where I stood. I looked at the ground again, confused, ashamed.

After a silence he spoke. I didn't seem to hear him clearly. He repeated himself. Then I understood. He spoke another language.

I searched in my memory. From the tours I had made with my father, I knew a lot of the dialects of this area, but none came close to what he had said. I tried a few words in one of the dialects, then in another. He looked questioning. I looked questioning.

I grew desperate. I had to find a way to talk with him!

Finally I spoke in the traders' language of the North, a course, inflexible tongue but the last one I hadn't tried yet—and haltingly he answered.

I don't remember exactly what we said. I was completely caught out by the goodness in his voice. I knew he was different from anybody I knew. We must have talked about commonplace things, like a place for him to sleep and something to eat, but I felt he was a wise man, someone who had gone through much suffering and who understood about Life. He would know about the world, about the stars and about He who created everything. I had been waiting for this man ever since my father died.

"I give you thanks," I said, looking in vain for better words in the primitive language that we were both haltingly using.

The other villagers had apparently accepted the girl's courageous intervention, and she had brought me to her house, a small, neat clay hut near the river. It was almost empty; there was only a water jug in a corner, a folded straw mat against the wall, and a few dried herbs hanging from the ceiling, which gave off a pleasant smell. In the wall opposite the entrance, there was a little fireplace with a chimney that allowed smoke to leave the hut.

She had made a small fire and from a niche in the wall, she had given me bread, and small orange tomatoes that were very sweet.

I was getting a more precise impression of her. She was eager to do something for me, but I felt at the same time, she kept a distance. And when I thanked her, my words didn't seem to register.

I drank the tea she made for me after the meal and felt her radiant eyes upon me. She was so happy I accepted her service. Her face was beaming. She had an inner beauty that I hadn't seen in anyone before.

She was a part of *Maya*, I reminded myself brusquely. The world around us was *Maya*, an illusion. Only God was real.

When she said that I could use her house for the night, I hesitated. This was always a difficult moment. As a monk, I could not sleep in the same house as a woman.

I had already explained to the girl I was a monk and I got the impression she had understood the concept. Maybe she would not be offended if I said I wanted to sleep somewhere else.

"Oh, but I will sleep outside," she said immediately when I started to talk, as if she had been planning that all along.

I objected that the nights were getting cold in this time of the year, but she wouldn't listen. She neatly arranged the mat for me on the floor and a jug of water beside it, added some wood to the fire and then left the hut.

Unexpectedly, after a minute or two, she came back. She turned to me, her eyes downcast, and after a considerable hesitation, she took a small flower from a pocket in her dress. She held it out to me, still without looking at me.

"My house, your house," she said in a ritual, singsong way. I felt paralyzed for a moment. I didn't know what to answer. Then, without thinking, I accepted the flower. She still didn't look up at me, but when she quickly left the hut, her face beamed, as if she was overflowing with light.

Of course I would never sleep in a house alone with a

man. Even *him* I didn't dare to trust so much yet. So I was glad he had a monk's rule about it and I could go to my hut in the tree.

But before I left, I did something that made my heart beat in my throat. I had served him a small meal—it was all I had—and made tea for him and he hardly said a word to me all that time. Still I felt how kind he was and how deep, and I became sure, so sure, that he was the one I had been waiting for. I wanted him to stay; I wanted to learn from him.

Finally I left my hut to go to my tree, but then I did this unheard-of thing. In an impulse that made me forget all decent behavior, I returned to my hut—and I offered him a flower with the ritual words.

And he accepted!

I was so happy. He would come back one day and I would serve him and I would learn from him and—and...

I'm still lying awake, on the wooden logs high in my tree. I've watched the stars for a long time and my thoughts keep going around and around. I have become afraid of what I am feeling for this stranger. When my father died, I promised myself I would never, never get attached to anyone again. It would hurt too much. And now I can't bear the idea of letting my monk go, tomorrow.

Autumn, Second Moon, eleventh day

This morning I got up before sunrise, as usual. I took a bath in the nearby river, meditated for an hour and then set out for the next village. In my bag, I carried a piece of the bread that the girl had given me the night before—and the flower.

I never kept anything of the things people gave me unless I had an immediate use for it, like food. But the flower had been given with such deep sincerity; and I couldn't forget her face overflowing with happiness when I accepted her offer.

"You are getting sentimental," I muttered. "What kind of monk are you?" But I kept the flower.

I walked a long distance this morning, over the plains that surrounded the village. Twice I saw a glimpse of a man with a wild beard and crazy eyes. In each case, he seemed to follow me for a while, running from bushes to bushes when he thought I didn't look. He never came near.

Many kilometers further, I saw signs that a *vielfrass* was around, or maybe more than one. *Vielfrass* were aggressive predators, when they were hungry, they didn't hesitate to attack lonely travelers. Of course it was all in God's hand what happened with me, but it was safer to be careful.

Just when the sun was setting, I reached a fast-flowing river. Normally I would have stayed the night on this side of the water, but now I wanted to have the river between the *vielfrass* and me. I saw that the water was deep at many places, and I was glad when I found a place where several stones in the river offered me a dry crossing. The stones were slippery, and in the fading light, it was difficult to see where I should put my feet. Half an hour later the crossing would have been dangerous, if not impossible.

Twice I almost fell, but finally I managed to reach the other side safely. Then I saw, in the last light of the day, that also here were footprints and droppings of a *vielfrass*.

Frustration or fear was not a feeling I ever entertained. I had left those feelings behind when I became a monk. I was tired but I simply decided not to sleep; I would meditate until sunrise. I collected wood, made a fire that would keep the animal at a distance, and sat down.

When I woke up, I realized I was lying on my back. I must have fallen asleep. My second impression was that of warm, stinking air in my face. I opened my eyes.

Just above me, I saw the sharp teeth of a *vielfrass*.

It growled from deep within his throat—it was going to attack.

I didn't move. I closed my eyes and tried to surrender to God. This was the end.

The next thing I became aware of was the sound of a thump, and a startled yelp from the *vielfrass*. A second thump followed. The stinking breath disappeared. I opened my eyes slightly. I saw the stars. The teeth had gone.

Slowly I rolled over and saw the *vielfrass* running away, slightly limping and yelping with fear.

Dazed, I sat up. "Thank you, oh God," I mumbled.

Then, in the light of the pale moon, I noticed the girl. She stood at a little distance, trembling, a big stone still in her hand.

And her clothes, her hair, everything was dripping wet.

He hardly seemed shaken by his close encounter with the *vielfrass*. He seemed only concerned about me. "You must be freezing," he said. "You're wet through."

He got up and took off his mantle.

He gave it to me and said, "Get out of your wet clothes and wrap yourself in my mantle. I'll collect wood for a new fire. I'll be back in a few minutes."

There was still enough wood lying around the remains of the old fire, but he disappeared behind a low hill and returned only a while later.

I waited until I couldn't see him any more, then changed clothes. His mantle was heavy with dirt on the outside, but the inside was clean and warm, and strange enough I felt peaceful when I had it around me. I settled down to wait for him, a few stones by my side, in case the *vielfrass* would come back. Idly, I looked at glowing embers of the fire. I thought about how narrow my monk's, er, *the* monk's escape had been. Had I hesitated one minute longer when I couldn't find a place to cross the river safely, he would have been dead. Still, he didn't seem shaken.

He returned with the wood. Expertly he put the

branches together in such a way that the fire would burn easily. Next he took one small piece of wood between his hands. He sat partly turned away from me, and I couldn't see more than that he closed his eyes for a while. Then I saw that the piece of wood was glowing and finally burst into flames. He put it quickly under the other wood and soon the fire was burning.

I didn't feel like thinking about this. I moved in close to get warmer.

Still I was shivering. The monk looked at me for a moment and took from his bag a small clay jar with a handle on the side. He filled it with leaves, also from his bag, and some water from his bottle. Through the handle, he put the longest stick he could find and used it to hold the jar in the fire.

"This tea will make you warm," he said.

I felt embarrassed. He went to so much trouble for me. *He* must be feeling cold now, without his mantle. The clothes he wore under it seemed quite thin. "I'm all right," I protested weakly. But I don't think he could believe me very much, with the clattering of my teeth.

"Here," the monk said soon after. "Drink up."

His words were curt but I heard the kindness behind them. I felt tears stinging my eyes.

I drank hastily. The tea was sweet and soothing. "Thank you," I said.

He looked at me and answered, "God sent you just in time."

He didn't say anything more until I finished my tea.

"Now sleep," he said. But he didn't need to tell me.

I stayed up the rest of the night. I had to keep the fire going and make sure the *vielfrass* didn't come back. For a while I tried to do meditation but instead, against my habit, I thought about the future. What plan of

God was unfolding now? I looked again and again at the girl's face, relaxed and trusting in her sleep. I wondered who she was. Was she as young as I thought? She didn't seem to have any parents or guardians.

Why had she come after me? Apparently, even the river, for me a difficult obstacle by daylight, hadn't been able to stop her at night. She had simply *swum*. Before that, she had braved the madmen on the plains. She hadn't even run away from the *vielfrass*.

God had sent her; that was clear. She had to rescue me from certain death. But what now? Would she go back? I didn't want her to stay around any longer than necessary, that was sure. Monks never had company. Certainly not girls.

I prayed to God for understanding and again tried to do meditation. But concentration eluded me.

Was this a test? I had been a monk for many years, always wandering from village to village, not attached to any person or any place. Never had I felt tempted to marry.

God wanted to teach me something with this situation, I was sure. But what? I had discarded all weaknesses and inner enemies long ago. For twenty years or more I had known neither fear nor anger, neither hatred nor attachment, neither pride nor self-doubt. Fame or power didn't interest me at all. Food held no attraction for me, nor did people. There was nothing in the world that could disturb me.

People called me a saint. I called them *Maya*, illusion. Neither praise nor scorn could touch me. I could not be affected by anything in the world—I knew nothing was real but God.

So what was left to be learned?

Autumn, Second Moon, two-hands-and-two-fingers'-day

When I opened my eyes, it took me a moment to realize where I was. Then I remembered the long day march, the flight for the *meandi,* the crossing of the river in the middle of the night and the near drowning, and the constant fear of wild animals.

And finally, when I wanted to give up, I had discovered both the monk and the *vielfrass*. I remembered how I'd suddenly had no fears and shyness. I had picked up heavy stones and hurled them at the animal with a fierceness I hadn't known I had. Only when the danger was over, had I become myself again.

Finally there had been the hidden kindness of the monk, the tea, his mantle, the fire...

"God sent you here," a voice near my head said. I smiled. How good to hear his voice in a world where I was never at ease with people.

"God sent you here," the monk repeated, "and where does He send you now?"

He sat down beside me. I sat up, my heart beating faster with this deeply spiritual monk so close to me. I felt I never needed to be afraid anymore.

Then the meaning of the question got through to me. *Where does He send you now?*

I got a shock. He wanted me to leave!

I felt such pain.

In confusion I blurted out, "No—wait—please—" and then I realized I was talking in my own language.

I put my hands over my eyes, wanted to be dead. I couldn't bear the idea that he rejected me.

I felt his calm presence near me. He didn't say anything. He gave me the time to answer.

Slowly I pulled myself together. I had to think in that other language, which we both spoke a bit.

"Master...please...I came for you. I want to learn..."

When she finally started to cry, I gave up. No friendly words could persuade her to leave me alone and return to her village. I considered going there myself and handing her over to somebody.

But something in her had touched me—I hated to admit it—and

made me hesitate. Not her tears. I cannot be manipulated by a woman's tears. But this girl wasn't trying to manipulate me. She turned away from me when she started crying, she tried to hide her despair.

I suddenly understood. She was the kind of person who always offered her help, but would never ask for it. She didn't expect anyone would want to help her.

Yet she came to me, to ask for my teaching that she feels she needs so much. She came to me in full faith that this request for help, maybe the first in many years, would be honored.

What would be the effect on her if I refused?

My hesitation ended suddenly when an idea crossed my mind. I would allow her to accompany me, and very soon she would understand that a monk's life was not what she expected it to be. Long meditations, long day marches, long silences. Discomfort, dangers, hunger and cold. Within three days, she would beg me to let her go home.

I am sure he doesn't like me. He doesn't want me as his student. But at first, he told me it was all right, and I was so happy. I said to myself again and again I would do everything for him I could, and I would never disturb him, never complain, never do *anything* that would make him annoyed with me.

By the time the sun had climbed to its highest point today, we had been walking for many hours without stopping or eating. My feet hurt from the long trek yesterday, the muscles in my legs protested at every step I took, and my monk hadn't spoken one word since he gave his slow "all right" early in the morning. It was clear he was not happy with me. I began to doubt my impulsive decision to leave everything and follow him.

The discomfort, the lack of food, the silence, I could bear all that. But the thought that with my presence I disturbed my Master's mood, his spiritual thoughts, this was impossible for me to stand. I told myself I was very selfish.

I struggled for many hours with this. He was the first person after my father whom I had trusted. He had given me so much kindness. He knew deep things that would make my life worthwhile at last. But still—I couldn't impose myself. My life was not important enough to disturb him.

Finally, with pain in my heart, I made a decision. I would tell him I was going back.

I walked faster than normal. Partly to make clear to this girl that this life was nothing for her, partly because I was disturbed by nagging thoughts and I tried to distance myself from them by strenuous walking.

Why had God sent her? He could have made someone else rescue me from the *vielfrass.* He could have made her go back to her village. He could have made her a humdrum girl without this inner beauty.

Ah. This was what bothered me most.

I had trained myself to be totally indifferent to female beauty, but what she had, was different. Her purity, her humbleness, the radiant light that shone in her eyes when she was happy—this was not physical beauty, this was beauty of a higher order.

I mulled this over. All right, it was not something low. This girl was something special. But still she was *Maya*, something created to lure people away from the path to God. Nothing material was real.

I kept walking; I kept thinking.

Oh God, I know You are testing me. I'll not give in. I'll be distant to her. I'll be unaffected. I'll…

I kept walking. Thoughts kept coming.

Suppose God sent her to show Himself through her? I thought of all the people I had met; was anybody so open as this girl? Everyone always had a big protecting wall around himself. None had trusted me so completely; in none the inner light had shone out so purely. She had such beautiful faith, such childlike innocence. Wasn't this truly divine?

But words from my guru welled up in me. "Don't look for God

anywhere except in your meditation. He is everywhere, but in material things, His image is distorted. Don't attach importance to anything in this world."

I had taken his words to heart. When I left the spiritual monastery, after years of austere training, I vowed I would not be attached to anything worldly, and not hindered by any emotion or other inner weakness. Hatred—a destructive force. Lust—foolishness of the body. Self-doubt—unnecessary. Jealousy—no reason for it. Who could take God away from me? Anger—why? Just accept whatever comes. Fear— of what? Everything was *Maya*. Pride—pride was the only one that had managed to trick me for a while. I had felt proud that others had pride and I didn't. But even that I had recognized and discarded. I didn't give any weakness the chance to manifest itself. I was in full control.

I looked at the girl, always a few paces behind me. She staggered sometimes; she had to be very tired. But she didn't say anything. For a moment I felt pity for her. But no I did not entertain such feelings.

For years nothing in this world had affected me, I thought. *But for years nothing in this world had shown me God*. And nothing in my meditation had shown Him to me either. My meditation had always been a searching, never a finding. "Look for God in your meditations," my Guru had said. He had never told me there would be many years when God didn't appear. And here—God sent me someone who mirrored His light so purely. Should I turn my back on His gift?

The plain gave way to a series of low hills. Here and there wild corn grew, and in between there were countless little plants that I didn't know. I paid no attention. I increased my pace. I had not felt so disturbed in years.

The moment I wanted to say I wouldn't disturb him any longer, the moment my mouth was forming the M of Master, my foot hit a stone and I stumbled. I couldn't stop myself, my other foot hit the ground at a wrong angle and a sharp pain went through my ankle. I fell.

"You cannot walk with this," I said, straightening up. I had inspected her ankle, touching her as little as possible, and found it was probably only sprained.

"I can," the girl said, trying to get up.

"You can*not,*" I said sternly.

With a sigh, she sank back. "Oh Master, don't let me bother you any longer. Please continue without me. I will go back to my village."

I almost smiled at the idea. She wouldn't be able to use that ankle at all for a few days. Even if she had a strong ankle, I should not let her go alone all the way back to her village. I had decided that earlier already. It was not a journey for a girl alone.

"Forget it," I said, almost unfriendly. "We are going to stay here. I'll make a bandage for your foot so it will not swell very much."

She surprised me by pointing at a small plant that was growing everywhere on these hills.

"I'll chew its leaves and cover my ankle with it," she said. "It will make it heal faster."

For a while we worked in silence. She prepared the paste for her foot. I tore off the long tough leaves of the wild corn that I found here and there, to make a bandage. When I finally wrapped the leaves tightly around her ankle, she looked at me gratefully with total surrender. I felt a very old and disturbing emotion: I was glad I could do something for her. And I felt guilty I had caused this all, by walking so fast.

The guilt I managed to get under control immediately. The gladness took a bit longer. Treating her injury and seeing her gratefulness gave me a fleeting sense of closeness to her. I knew how futile that was, and how dangerous. It wouldn't bring me any closer to God—on the contrary. But it was so tempting, this warm feeling of being close to someone, of being open. I hadn't felt it for years and years.

I'd never known I missed it. The girl was already spoiling me!

I tried to be angry with her and found I couldn't.

She started to talk again. "Master, I'm very sorry, I'm such a burden for you, please leave me here... You are in a hurry and I'm keeping you, please go..."

I felt again a sharp twinge of guilt when she said, "You are in a hurry."

"I'm not going anywhere, child," I said gruffly. "Stop whimpering."

She looked shocked for a moment, then seemed to accept that she deserved my gruffness.

Another twinge of pain went through me.

"It's not your fault, my child," I managed to say more friendly now. "I walked too fast. Sorry." I reflected how strange these words were for me. I hadn't said "sorry" for years and meant it.

I sat down besides her and hid my deep disturbance over my feelings and behavior by digging in my bag. I came up with some berries. "Here, you must be hungry."

She gratefully accepted them, but when she wanted to put them in her mouth, her eyes went wide and she looked at the ground, clearly ashamed. "Please, you eat first, Master," she said.

A few moments we sat there, chewing the sour berries. I tried not to look at her, but the peace and happiness that radiated from her were too beautiful to resist.

"My child," I said to distract myself, "what is your name?"

Autumn, Second Moon, four-hands' day

He insisted on calling me Gem. That is not at all my real name, but he said it described my spiritual qualities. I don't know what it means; it's a word from his own language.

Maybe he will explain it later to me. But if he wants to call me Gem I'm very happy. I'll wear the name with pride and gladness. It's a sign for me that he has accepted me. Maybe this is his way of giving the flower of connectedness? I don't dare to ask.

I didn't ask his name. I call him *Master*. I feel he is not completely the spiritual Master I thought he was, grave and imperturbable. But surely I want to accept him as my Master. Actually, I feel closer to him now I have seen he is not perfect. Isn't that funny? Of course I should not tell him this.

If he doesn't call me *Gem*, he calls me *my child*. I know I look young, but do I look that young? Maybe this is the first thing I learn from my Master.

I never wanted to grow up and leave my family. But my family was taken from me, first my mother when I was eight, then my father when I was fourteen.

At that age, it was time for me to marry, but I didn't want to. I refused. The others in the village gossiped about me at every occasion, hurting me. But I wouldn't change my mind. I could not marry because I still wanted to be a child.

And there was another thing. Even before the sooth-sayer came and predicted my future, I knew I had to remain free; free for something that would happen later. I didn't know what. I only knew I would never marry.

So I withdrew from the other villagers and lived alone all these harvests.

I still don't want to marry. But I always wanted a new father.

I have found him.

Autumn, Second Moon, twenty-sixth day

We travel from village to village. She always walks two steps behind me and she never asks for rest or food. Even when I ask her if she is tired, she will say "no", although often I can see she is exhausted. She is not used to so much walking. I cannot understand how she made that long trek the first day when she traveled alone, to catch up with me.

When I announce a pause and a meal between two villages, she hurries to collect wood for the fire or find food or do whatever else is needed, while I do my meditation. When she has nothing more to do, she just sits and waits.

There's no fidgeting, no unrest. She sits completely motionless and passive and looks like she would remain like that even when I did meditation for twenty-four hours.

Sometimes it irritates me she is like that. Does she have no wishes for herself? Is there nothing she wants to do except serve me? Of course a monk is not irritated. I will find another word for it.

At the same time, I am trying to figure out *why* it, er, irritates me. *This* also irritates me. After being an imperturbable monk for more than twenty years, I am compelled to analyze my feelings.

I shouldn't *have* any.

Autumn, Second Moon, five-hands-and-two-fingers' day

When we are walking between two villages, my Master remains silent. I find this sometimes difficult, because there is so much I want to ask him. But maybe the silence is good for me. If my Master does it, I want to do it, too.

I try to think about nothing, because thoughts are almost as noisy as talk, I feel. But it's really hard. My mind is restless; I always think of many things.

Today I remembered the visit of the soothsayer to our village. She must have known about my Master.

It happened a few moons ago. She was a young woman with dirty black clothes, a thin face with narrow black eyes, and long, matted black hair. She carried a bulky green bag on her back. She swept into our village shouting strange words at the dogs that were running around her, and they all became quiet and slunk away.

In the center of our village she stopped, grabbed the first man she saw by his arm and demanded to see our chief. When he came, she told him she could cure diseases, remove warts and tell people's fortune. And she said that she would stay only one day, so everyone better hurry up.

Our chief didn't like the way she talked. He started to tell her off in a loud voice. All villagers came and watched.

And she, she just stared at the chief. At first, he kept talking, but after a while, he started to stammer and stutter, and finally, he fell still, lowering his gaze.

He couldn't do anything about it. There was fire in the eyes of the soothsayer. I saw that only later, because when the others crowded around her, I stayed in my tree hut and kept my distance.

She demanded food and drink, and when that had been brought, she sat down in the grass under my tamarind tree. I looked at her from above and saw how she began to treat the people. She took many different kinds of cream from her bag and muttered dark words while she smeared them on warts, wounds and infected fingers. If people wouldn't pay her with enough skins or bone knives or other things that were beautiful, she would scold them furiously and threaten to cast a spell on them.

For some she predicted the future. She would suddenly grab a patient's hand when he was about to get up, and force him to stay and listen. She had a bowl that seemed to be filled with water, only the water was solid although it was spring, and she peered into that bowl and said she saw there what would happen with the people.

"You are in love with a girl with a scar on her temple— but be careful! You will have to fight with someone to get her. I can give you something to increase your strength..."

"You say you want to be the next chief of the village. But it's your wife's wish and not yours. She always talks and talks to you, doesn't she? Wait—with this amulet you can make her silent by just looking at her..."

"You will get badly hurt in the next hunt. But if you wear this black scarf for three nights in a row and you give me some of your hair for an incantation..."

Beside her, she collected the things the scared villagers gave her, and the pile grew and grew.

Suddenly she stood up and shooed away the waiting people. "I'm tired!" she exclaimed. "Leave me alone until tonight!"

When the people left her, disappointed and relieved at the same time, she suddenly looked up and saw me in the tree.

"Who are you?" she demanded. "Come down!"

I trembled, but my hands and feet obeyed her automatically. A few moments later, I stood in front of her. I saw how her black eyes burned. I noticed a strange, slightly sour smell coming from her. It was not from lack of regular washing. It was a sourness I had never smelled before. I thought it came from her mind.

"And what do *you* need?" she snapped.

"I have nothing to give in return." I said, my voice shaking a bit.

She looked hard at me. Her eyes burned into mine. It hurt, but I couldn't tear myself loose.

"What's your name?" she demanded.

I told her.

"That will change soon," the soothsayer said. She kept looking at me. "You are *strange,*" she added. She shook her head.

"I see that you will never marry, but soon you will live with two men."

I felt shocked. I tried not to hear her and looked at the frozen water bowl that lay on the ground, unused.

"That's a toy!" she snarled. She pushed it away with

her foot. "Just like the creams. I don't need them!"

She searched my face and her black eyes became narrower. "When you are older, you'll be called a mother, but you will not nurse any children."

I squirmed.

"You will be loved by many!" she exclaimed. She scowled furiously. "Why will they love you? *I* don't like you at all!"

I shook my head and took a step backwards, away from her.

The soothsayer grabbed my wrist. "You have to tell me! What makes you so special? What do you want to do with your life?"

I could not escape from her fierce grip.

I opened my mouth, but I couldn't make a sound. Finally, I managed to whisper, "Nothing—nothing... I just want to understand why we are living—and where we are going..."

The woman didn't say anything. Once more, she looked intently at me. She didn't quite focus, it seemed; she was staring at something around me or beyond me.

Then her face changed. The harshness dropped from it; she looked almost vulnerable. She let go of my wrist.

"I have seen more of your future," she said. "I want to tell you about it... No need to give me anything for it."

My body stopped trembling. I kept looking at her face, suddenly so much younger than before.

She took a deep breath. "I'm sorry. I am so nasty. It's because you are like me. But you are stronger than I."

She sat down heavily on the grass and after a moment, I sat down as well.

She looked into my eyes and seemed to ask something. I relaxed. I didn't understand what she had told me, but I understood what her eyes said. She felt lost. She wanted help.

I gave her a little smile.

She said slowly, "I see you have big questions. About life. About where everything came from, and *why* we are living."

She took a deep breath. "I—I once asked the same questions. I was burning to know the answers. But I didn't try hard enough to get the right answers. I was satisfied with small stuff I learned. I became—well, you see what I am. I make warts disappear and frighten people with predictions and silly spells. All I have is some occult powers.

"But you... I see you will spend a lifetime trying to get answers. You will work, and wait, and learn. And in the end—in the end you'll get the real answers."

She closed her eyes for a moment. "Answers that I can't describe."

Then she looked at me again. "I see you'll be a teacher, too. You'll—you will..."

She stopped and shook her head. "I cannot under-stand your life. You will be nothing... You will be every-thing. You will have immense powers, but you will not need them. Because you will be one with—one with—"

She swallowed with difficulty. I couldn't see if she was angry or sad. Abruptly she stood up and turned around. With brusque movements she put her bowl and creams in her bag, and then she walked away quickly, her head bowed. All the things the villagers had given her, she left behind.

Now it is several moons later. I still remember her strange sour smell. And her face—the longing in her eyes, in the end.

I still don't understand most of the things she said. Or

what she wanted to tell me when she didn't finish her sentence.

I wonder if I will ever see her again. I would like to. She wasn't a bad person. Maybe one day I can help her.

Autumn, Second Moon, five-hands-and-three-fingers' day

I'm sure my Master is perfect. Maybe he even pretends to be impatient; it must be a way to teach me. Maybe it's for all the things I did wrong before. I'm willing to accept everything he does. I cannot know what is good for me and what is not; I will just try to serve him as well as I can.

Autumn, Third Moon, fifth day

Actually, it is practical she is with me. I can't understand the local dialects at all, and whenever we are in a village, she translates. Lately she even does all the talking without my prompting.

This region is difficult. In the north, where I came from, people know what a monk is and respect me. Here they don't.

Gem has turned out to be a great diplomat; she knows how to take away the suspicion of the villagers when they see my wild beard and bald head. Or maybe she is simply herself and convinces the people with her vibration. They are happy to see her and take me into the bargain.

Sometimes her task is not easy. Villagers wonder why this so-called monk is traveling with a girl, and sometimes they try to separate us. That is, they throw me out. When that had happened twice—of course Gem followed me into exile—she did something that must have been a great sacrifice for her. She let me cut off her beautiful long hair.

It pained me to do it…

Next, she got herself a set of boy's clothes from a friendly woman in one of the villages, including a gaily colored mantle that is too big for her, and now at first sight she looks like a boy. Of course her high voice betrays her, and also the whole, subtle atmosphere she creates around her by just being herself. Yet her sacrifice helps us; we encounter less suspicion in the villages.

At first, I felt embarrassed when I impulsively called her "Gem". Now I am convinced she deserves the name.

Autumn, Third Moon, three-hands' day

My Master is such a special person. In many villages, the people don't recognize that he is a spiritual person; they believe in all kinds of gods and sacrificial offerings and don't understand my Master. But he never complains. He always behaves in a grave, dignified manner. I'm sure some of the people who see him will realize later that they met a special person.

And then, as soon as we have left a village, my Master changes. I don't want to say he isn't still dignified, but he somehow becomes a bit more relaxed, more free. He talks a little more, he smiles sometimes, he eats more than the little bits he takes when other people are around. I feel very happy when he changes like this. He feels more at ease with me. As if I am part of the family.

I have a family again, can you imagine...!

Sometimes we are far away from a village when the sun sets. In that case, we sleep in the open field. My Master is careful to give me privacy, both with sleeping and with bathing.

He cares for me; when the night is cold, he gives me his mantle and he sleeps without. In the beginning I felt embarrassed—why would he suffer for a person like me?—but he said he doesn't feel the cold. He learned ways, a *mantra*, he calls it, to keep himself always warm or cool, just as he wishes. I understand now that the fire I always make for us is actually only for me... Only sometimes we need it to keep the wild animals away.

I wonder if I can learn this *mantra*. But first, I want to learn what he does when he meditates. I don't dare to ask him, though. I don't want to bother him.

There are so many things I would like to ask him. Who made the world? Where did we come from? What happens after we die? Often, when my Master is doing meditation, I think about these questions.

Autumn, Third Moon, seventeenth day

I got a thorn in my foot and I walk with some difficulty. Gem noticed it—I think there is little that escapes her, although she rarely talks about what she thinks—and she urged me to rest and let the wound heal. To humor her, I walk only in the mornings. For me the pain doesn't matter. The body hurts, but the body is not me.

Usually we don't talk. When I walk, I never want to speak. I want to keep my mind empty. Now we have whole afternoons until dusk when we don't walk. I feel Gem is burning to learn things, so today I started to teach her. I told her about the three aspects of our existence: the physical, the mental and the spiritual.

I remember more and more of the traders' language that we are using, and I can express myself quite well by now. Gem seems to know at least as much as I do. We only have to invent some new words, every now and then, such as for "spiritual" and "mental", which neither of us had ever heard in that language.

I have no idea what Gem understands. She never interrupts, never asks a question; she just listens, with those radiant eyes fixed on me.

I told her we should not waste mental or spiritual energy in solving physical problems, such as, we should not cure a person's physical disease with occult powers when herbs will also make him better. Spiritual powers should only be used to bring us closer to God. A disease should only be cured if it is an obstacle on our way to Him. This thorn in my foot doesn't really disturb me—pain is easy to ignore—so if it were not for Gem I would just continue walking the full length of the day.

Gem drinks in every word I say. She always beams when I give her attention, but now when I talk about spiritual things, the intense joy her face radiates is so beautiful that I cannot look at it. I usually gaze up at the sky when I talk to her, and I'm sure she takes it for a kind of spiritual rapture.

For the rest, I don't know what she thinks. Maybe she didn't understand anything of what I told her. I wish she would tell me what is going on in her mind.

I'm so happy! My Master has started teaching me! I tried to understand everything he told me this afternoon, about spiritual energy, occult powers and not doing physical things with it. It all seemed very natural to me, as if I had always lived with this knowledge. But at the same time I was thrilled to hear it again. It was as if my Master dug up treasures for me that I had hidden in the earth long ago.

I understand now why the soothsayer felt so bad with her life.

Only one thing I didn't understand; I'll have to disturb him and ask about it...

Autumn, Third Moon, nineteenth day

Gem is changing. The other day she forgot her deep respect for me for a moment and indirectly criticized me!

Usually it is she who collects the wood, and then I make the fire. I always do that by generating much body heat and concentrating it all in one hand and then in one finger, and if I hold a small piece of wood it will start glowing and finally burning. It's nothing special, a bit of concentration on the shape and sound of a *chakra*.

Gem has seen me do it many times. I recently explained her how it works, and she didn't comment on it. But this time she asked, "Master, aren't you using spiritual energy to do something physical?"

I was so surprised that I didn't know what to say. She was right. I had been making fire like this for years and never thought about it. Who knows what other intelligent thoughts are hidden behind her silence!

After that, we carried a couple of small firestones with us that produced sparks if you hit them against each other. Given patience and practice, you can make fire with it. Gem taught me how to do it—*she* was teaching *me*! I'm glad I can say I was only a little bit embarrassed. Of course monks are not embarrassed, but—well. I'm coming close to the point when I accept that she is disturbing my whole life. I have an inkling that God wants it this way. Although only He knows why.

If there is strong wind on the plains that blows out any beginning fire, we make the fire together. She clashes the firestones against each other over a splinter of wood, and I hold my bigger hands around hers and the wood to keep the wind out. We make the fire together.

The first time it affected me to be so close to someone physically, and I was slow in suppressing the warm feeling it gave me. I looked at her serious, concentrated face while we tried to make the wood glow, and marveled again at her inner beauty. How could I think she was fourteen, or even twenty? She clearly has the depth of a thirty-year-old.

Autumn, Third Moon, four-hands-and-two-fingers' day

"Master, excuse me for asking you, but what are you doing when you meditate?"

My Master looked gravely at me and said nothing for a while. Then he slowly nodded and asked, "Do you know who God is?"

My father told me sometimes about God, He who made the world and the stars, He who was so vast nobody could understand Him. I used to try to imagine Him, feeling a bit ashamed that in that way I didn't have enough respect for His vastness—and at the same time feeling thrilled to be thinking about something *so* big.

"I heard that God is the one who made everything, Master."

"Yes," he said slowly. God is...God is an infinite Entity and He is pure love. Now do you understand Him?"

My Master sometimes sounds quite stern when he explains something. I try to understand everything the first time so he doesn't get angry with me. So I said, "Yes, Master," with a little twinge of guilt because I didn't speak the truth.

"Hmmm," my Master said. He didn't sound quite convinced. But he continued, "Now, to meditate is to open yourself for God and to become one with Him. Meditation is *not* asking favors from God; 'Dear God, destroy my enemies, dear God, give me a good harvest this time.'

"Meditation is a silent listening to what God is."

Was this what I had done, as a child? I didn't know.

I asked another thing that was on my mind.

"You often look happy, Master, after your meditation," I said.

My Master smiled. "You'll understand that later."

"Oh, do you mean..." A wave of happiness rolled through me. "Do you mean that I can also learn meditation?"

My Master looked at me gravely, probingly.

"Later," was all he said.

Autumn, Third Moon, twenty-second day

I waver between being more open to her and keeping a sphinx-like reserve. Sometimes I cannot stop myself and call her "Gem". Usually I manage to say "my child" and keep a safe distance.

I'm always aware of her, see her out of the corner of my eye, feel her childlike purity and the miracle of her trust in me. Never have I seen such divine light pouring out of someone, not even my Guru. He kept his divine light hidden. Gem is totally open.

Oh, why did God manifest Himself in somebody I cannot be close to? Why does God torture me in this way? I long for the peaceful days when I wandered alone through the lands, without distraction, without feelings, without really seeing anything or anyone. All were *Maya*, to be ignored as much as possible. I had peace. My feelings were safely beneath the surface until I believed that they didn't exist.

The only problem was that I didn't see You, my God. That was the price I had to pay for having no feelings. And now I see You, but You chose a form I can't be close to…

Autumn, Third Moon, twenty-ninth day

"Gem, what is the advantage of being unimportant?"

She looked at me with uncomprehending eyes.

"You are not important, you tell me so often."

"Yes, Master." She looked at the ground.

"Have you ever imagined being important?"

She seemed to study the ground even more intently. "That would be wrong, Master," she said in a barely audible voice.

"Ah," I said. "You mean, that would be nice. Wouldn't it?"

"Master, I am *not* important," she said with an almost desperate emphasis.

I smiled. "I know, I know, Gem. That has been your choice. Other people do less good than you do, yet they consider themselves more important than others. You insist you are less important than the rest of the world. So I ask you, what is the advantage this gives you?"

She sent me a blank look.

"Can you finish this sentence, Gem," I said, looking kindly at her. *"As long as I am unimportant, I don't need to…"*

She remained silent for a while, blinking her eyes. Then suddenly she blushed and looked at the ground.

"See…" I said.

"No Master.…er, yes, Master," she stammered, "but please, let's not talk about me." She turned away, hid her face. I felt sorry for her. But I felt I had to confront her with this. "Gem," I said with gentle insistence.

"I have to make fire, Master," she answered quickly, and without waiting for an answer, she disappeared to collect wood.

Autumn Third Moon, six-hands' day

"Master," I asked today, "Where are we going?"

My Master looked at me with his usual grave expression. He didn't answer.

I thought about this. Maybe he didn't know?

I had asked myself this question before. Why did wandering monks wander?

Because my Master didn't answer, I started to think more deeply.

After a while I got an idea. "Master, is the journey the goal?" I asked timidly. Maybe this was a very stupid idea. I don't know how it came to my mind.

I thought I saw a flicker of a smile on my Master's face. However, he slightly shook his head.

We continued walking, and I continued thinking about the question.

After half an hour, I came up with a new idea. "Master, is our journey...to God?" I asked eagerly. This had to be the right answer.

But my Master remained silent. I became confused.

"Are we then *not* on the way to God?" I asked, finally.

Again, I received silence as an answer. We continued walking for more than an hour.

I gave up. "I don't understand your teaching," I said. I felt frustrated, but of course I shouldn't have been. I tried to be more humble and respectful. "Master," I added.

I thought my Master would again be silent, but after a few moments he spoke. "You ask, are we on our way to God," he said meditatively. "But where is God?"

He paused, as if waiting for an answer.

"God is everywhere," he said finally. "Isn't He? So we

cannot be on our way to God. The previous village was a manifestation of God. The next village is a manifestation of God. The road is God. We are walking on God from God to God. We are always in God." Again, he was silent, and I tried to understand his words.

"Everything is a manifestation of God. I am a manifestation of God. *You*, Gem," he stopped walking and turned to me, and for a moment I thought he wanted to take my face in his hands, "you are a manifestation of God."

After what seemed to be a very long silence he started walking again. My cheeks glowed, as if he had really touched me.

He walked fast, at first, then he slowed down. He looked at me for a moment. "So you see, we are with God all the time. We don't need to go to Him."

I nodded slowly, trying to digest these new thoughts. "The only thing we need to do," my Master said, and he cleared his throat, "is to learn to see Him around us."

We walked for a long time, crossed a ravine, walked along a river until we found a shallow place and struggled through a forest of blackberry bushes that stung and clung to us. The sun began to set.

"So you wonder why we are walking," my Master said abruptly.

I nodded quickly, ready to drink in every word. My Master's face suddenly opened up and lost his graveness, his lips twisted into a smile.

"Force of habit, maybe," he said.

She could never guess what was going on in my mind, when she asked about the goal of our wandering. A monk is supposed to wander so that he doesn't get attached to *Maya*, the great illusion that man calls "world".

From the beginning, I was aware that this world is an illusion. I kept myself at a great distance from it. On my journeys, I saw many a majestic mountain, countless colorful sunsets, innumerable people, plants and animals. I never let their beauty get through to me. For me they were gray objects, useful or useless, to be approached or avoided.

On my travels, I met so many people, young and old, male and female, helpful and hostile. I was kind to them or I endured them—but never did I let myself be affected by them. They were an expression of *Maya,* the misleading force that tries to turn people away from God with tempting colors, shapes and sounds.

I moved amongst things, and if I had to, I moved amongst people, but I always remained in a tiny world of my own, never opening up to anyone.

And then God sent me Gem. She radiated such purity and innocence that I could not avoid seeing she was an expression of God. And then slowly I understood that the world may be an illusion, but it is an illusion created by God. The world is a manifestation of God.

I should see the world's beauty. I should *enjoy* the world's beauty. Because in every object and every person I can see God. In meditation, I try to find God in His infinite form. In the world, I find God in His myriad of finite forms. Both are God.

Winter, First Moon, five-fingers' day

It's real winter now. I feel cold all the time. We try to sleep in villages, but it is not always possible. My Master feels cold, too. I think he has stopped using his mantra to keep himself warm. I did something wrong when I asked him why he used the mantra for fire making. It's my fault that he is freezing now.

Winter, First Moon, ninth day

Some creatures show more of God's beauty, love and limitlessness than others. In a flower, I can see a more subtle expression of Him than in a stone; in a person I see a more subtle manifestation of Him than in the flower. And in Gem—in Gem I can see God more purely than in anything else.

But this means I don't want to lose her. It makes me attached to her. It makes me bound by *Maya*—and that's the worst thing a monk can do to himself.

I wish I could talk about it with her.

What a crazy thought.

Winter, First Moon, all-fingers' day

"Master, I would like so much to learn meditation."

I thought my Master would say "no", or "later", like before, but he had just come back from his evening meditation on a nearby hilltop and his eyes sparkled and his face radiated deep bliss.

"Sure Gem, I'll be happy to teach you," he answered kindly. "But you know that it is a serious thing, to learn meditation?"

"I'll be very serious, Master." Oh, how I longed to be like him, blissful, peaceful, balanced. I was ready to do anything for that. Getting up early, sitting an hour in the cold, remaining hungry until I finish meditation, *anything*.

"Well Gem, sit down please. Are you ready for a long explanation?"

"Yes, Master."

"Are you hungry?"

"N-no, Master."

"Better be sure about that, my child."

"I don't mind the hunger, Master," I said quickly. "Are *you* hungry?"

"We are going to have mental food," my Master said. He sat down too, closed his eyes a moment and then looked very seriously at me.

"In the past," he said slowly, "spiritual aspirants had to prove they were able to lead a moral and exemplary life for twelve years, before they could learn meditation."

I tried to suppress a gasp. Twelve harvests!

"Nowadays," my Master continued, "people have less patience. Yet, they have to be willing to be good people, before they learn meditation. Meditation gives you a lot of mental power, and you have to be sure that you will not misuse it."

"I don't want to harm anybody, Master!" I said, shocked.

My Master looked at me affectionately. "I know that, Gem. But there is more to it than you realize. I've known you now for a little while. You are a very sweet and helpful girl."

My whole body trembled. Such praise! My Master had never said such things to me before.

"Yet," my Master continued, "I have seen you harm someone quite a few times."

I gasped. "*What*?" I even forgot to say "Master."

"Yes, my child. Do you remember that you were roasting carrots over our fire, the other day?"

My mouth fell open. "But they were *carrots*, Master!"

"No, my child, that's not what I mean. You dropped two of the carrots you were roasting into the fire."

"Yes, I'm sorry Master, I was careless. I gave the rest of the carrots to you, to punish myself for this mistake."

"Well, there you are, Gem," my Master said. "Suppose *I* had dropped the carrots. Would you want that I ate nothing?"

"No, of course not, Master!"

"Would you blame me for wasting those two carrots?"

"No, surely not, Master!"

"I'm glad, Gem. But then why did you judge and punish yourself for it?"

I blinked. Wasn't it obvious? "But Master, that's

different. It's—"

My Master looked at me with compassionate eyes.

"Now that's what I mean, Gem. You wouldn't harm a fly, I know. But you harm yourself sometimes. Or should I say, many times?"

I looked at the ground. I knew I had done something wrong, but I didn't understand what. I thought it was right to blame myself. My Master said it wasn't. But I *did* do something stupid. I do all the time. I'm careless. I forget things. I don't understand things quickly enough. I'm not doing enough for him...

My Master seemed to understand my thoughts. "Or should I say, you are harming yourself *all* the time? Aren't you judging, blaming, hurting yourself continuously?"

I took a deep breath and let the air out again slowly. I looked even harder at the ground than before. I wanted to sink through it. See how bad I was! I was even worse than I thought!

"Gem," my Master said, and just with the gentleness in his voice he lifted my chin and made me look into his eyes full of love. "Gem, I want you to understand that you are a very special girl. You have so much goodness in you. The only thing missing is that you don't know this."

I felt like crying. Since my father died, I hadn't cried except when my Master said I couldn't follow him. "But Master, I *am* bad! Honestly, I am! You don't know how bad I am!" My voice shook. "How can I be *friendly* to myself?"

My Master looked at me so full of kindness. I felt my despair lessen.

"Gem, trust me," he said. Just the sound of his voice made the bad feelings about myself go to the background. "Gem, I've met many people. I understand how they are, even when they try to hide their character.

"Now I know you very well. I said already, you are a very special girl. How special, you will soon discover. But for now think about this: In more than twenty years I have never allowed anybody to accompany me. A companion, a disciple, anybody would disturb me. But for you I gladly make an exception."

I looked at my Master, bursting with joy, doubting, confused, all quickly after each other.

"Meditate on this, tonight," my Master said after a silence. "We'll sleep here at the foot of this hill. Tomorrow we'll continue about the meditation."

When I woke up this morning, I noticed I had cried in my sleep. Fragments of happy dreams were still in my mind. When dawn came and brought a little warmth, we sat down together and my Master taught me a secret meditation technique that I promised to use every day at least twice.

The first time we did meditation together, I will always remember. I was lifted up beyond the sky, beyond the stars, to a place where there was only love. For the first time in ten, fifteen harvests, I stopped condemning myself.

My feeling of relief was indescribable. The rest of the day, I didn't say a word. I couldn't concentrate on anything. I drifted in bliss. I stared into the distance all the time and just smiled.

My Master told me later that he, too, smiled the whole day.

Winter, First Moon, seventeenth day

It is very cold. We are almost at the shortest day of the year, and even when the sun shines, water remains solid. The plains are white with frost and the trees have no leaves. It is difficult to dig up roots from the frozen ground. Our breath smokes when it leaves our mouths and the air bites our faces.

We don't feel it. While we are walking, I give long discourses to Gem, every day. My habitual silence I have broken. She listens intently; she even asks questions. Sometimes she corrects me. "But Master, yesterday you said…"

We must have passed villages on our way, but I don't remember any of them. I am only aware of Gem and me absorbed in spiritual philosophy in the day, and Gem and me sleeping by the fire at night. We don't think about what others would think if they saw us. We don't feel like a monk and a girl, we feel like two souls.

Sometimes in the early morning, the fire has gone out and I wake up hearing Gem's peaceful breathing so near me. A deep silence spreads in me at these moments, a sense of timelessness, a feeling that this moment will never change.

Winter, First Moon, four-hands-and-four-fingers' day

Our meditations are wonderful. Such peace I feel, such happiness…

Sometimes we meditate for more than an hour. Sometimes I continue after my Master has stopped. My back aches, my feet sleep and my knees hurt so much that afterwards I can't walk for quite a while. But it's worth it!

My Master has warned me that meditation is like cleaning your house. You will find a rotting apple and a broken jar in a corner and maybe a bunch of straw with a thick layer of mould on it. But when you have thrown these all out, the hut looks clean and nice and it's a joy living in it.

When I had a house, I never let it become a mess, but I understand what my Master means. Through meditation, I will see the parts of me that are bad, that I tried to hide from myself. And then I will admit they are there, and then I will throw them out.

I haven't noticed this yet, though. I just wish my Master would help me dig out the roots we collect for the meals. All he does is tell me where to look for them and *I* have to do the heavy work of getting them out of the ground.

Winter, First Moon, twenty-fourth day

I felt Gem was unhappy when she was digging up the roots we are eating every day. I guess she wants something else for a change, but nothing else edible grows here. We tried grass, but it upset our stomachs.

So one day, when I spotted a rabbit, I took a stone and with a lucky throw I hit the animal. It was unconscious and proudly I brought it to Gem, who was busy digging out the roots with a pointed stick, her small body in the oversized mantle bent over the holes in the ground. She hadn't noticed yet that we were going to have something special for dinner.

By the time I reached her, the rabbit had started moving again but it couldn't escape from my grip.

"Oh, Master," Gem said, straightening up, "did you find a sick rabbit?" She wanted to take it in her arms.

"Careful," I said, following my own thoughts, "don't let it escape, or we will eat only your roots tonight."

Gem's eyes became very big. Her cheeks flushed. "What?" she exploded. "You want to eat this poor animal?"

"Well, yes..." I said, completely taken aback. I had thought she would be happy. Rabbit or pheasant was something I ate only a few times in a year, when it was winter and there was nothing else to get.

"Let him go immediately!" Gem exclaimed. "Don't you see he's trembling all over? He is afraid! He wants to live!"

"But Gem," I said reasonably. "It's only a rabbit. And it's *Maya*. It's not real. This all is God's play, remember."

Her eyes were blazing. "I would rather eat roots for a month than killing this poor animal! Maybe he's *Maya* for you, but he's real for himself! He is suffering! Give him to me!"

Totally astounded by her outburst, I let her take the animal. It stopped wriggling as soon as it was in her hands and I watched how she stroked its head softly and finally put it on the ground. It looked up at her for a moment and then hopped off unhurriedly, looking back twice.

"What then did you eat in your village?" I asked her weakly, in an attempt to save face.

"Bread," she said curtly, "Milk. Vegetables. Fruits."

"Nobody ate meat?" I asked, incredulous.

"Yes, the others," she said, with contempt.

That night neither of us wanted to eat and we slept several meters away from each other. I kept hearing Gem's angry voice, "Maybe he's *Maya* for you, but he's real for himself!"

I have never felt as bad as I felt that night.

When the sun rose pale and without warmth over the nearby hills, I woke up to find Gem looking at me. I looked away in shame.

After a whole night of thinking, I realized I had never wanted to feel the suffering of others, people or animals. When I came to villages and they gave me food, I never thought twice if it was meat. I was eating *Maya* to maintain my body that was *Maya*. If people asked me for help, I would give it, but without feeling.

They are *Maya*, I always told myself. I was kind to them when appropriate, but I was never involved. I didn't let suffering of others touch me.

Only when I met Gem did I begin to really feel something for someone. It is confusing and often painful. But I've begun to under-stand that it is good. Sometimes I realize it's helping me to feel something for God. Since I'm accompanied by Gem, my meditation is much deeper. It's not a dry technique anymore. In meditation, I sometimes truly feel surrounded by love...and I want to answer that love.

The next morning it was I who dug up the roots for our breakfast. I hoped she understood I felt too much ashamed to say "I'm sorry".

Winter, First Moon, five-hands-and-two-fingers' day

I feel very confused about yesterday. How could my Master...? But I feel also very ashamed. How could I shout at him?

I still think I was right. But of course, I shouldn't have shown that.

Or was it all right, to save the rabbit?

I don't understand how I could burst out like that. It was terrible.

My Master told me once that meditation will change me. If that's the cause for my disrespectful behavior yesterday, I must stop meditating...

Winter, Second Moon, tenth day

"We'd better not go to this village, Master," Gem told me one evening when we approached a set of huts by the river. "I know these people. They are heathens and barbarians."

She told that the villagers had chased her and her father out of there when they had tried to sell their merchandise.

I felt quite confident that evening and also quite cold, temperatures still being close to the freezing point when the sun was under the horizon. I shrugged off her words. "They'll not do anything to us, Gem. Be confident. Otherwise you'll never achieve anything in life."

I saw her swallow and she made an attempt to square her shoulders. "Yes, Master," she said meekly. I felt vaguely annoyed. After the, er, incident with the rabbit, she had been trying even harder than before to be humble. It was really time she learned to show her teeth. I mulled it over for a few minutes and then lapsed into one of my "you better listen" speeches.

"Look here, Gem," I said and saw her raise her face to mine expectantly.

"You want to be humble?"

"Yes, Master, I would like to."

"Good," I said. "But you see, you have to be able to be the opposite first."

"Oh… But why, Master? I could never do that!"

"Then you have to understand what humbleness is. It is not that you say "yes" and "sorry" to everybody who walks over you because you think you are nothing. Real humbleness can come only when you feel you are just as important as everybody else. Understand? If you have decided to feel like that, you can start to think some other people maybe know more than you, or have more experience."

I nodded at her, feeling pleased with the explanation I was giving.

"If people criticize you for something you did, you have to think, 'whether I'm right or wrong, I'm a good, worthwhile person.' And then you look at what they said and you decide if there is something useful in it. And if there is, you thank them and try to use their advice. *That*'s humbleness.

"But never think you are useless. You are a child of God, and everything God made has great value. Understood?"

Gem's face had changed from meek to happy. "Yes, Master," she said with radiant eyes.

"But, Gem, you should look carefully to whom you are humble. Many people don't deserve your humbleness. Don't think that humbleness means you have to be nice and sweet all the time. Sometimes you need to growl and hiss. Let me tell you the story about the giant snake that…"

I was interrupted by a harsh voice from out of the darkness. We had already reached the first huts of the village; I had been talking with so much inspiration that I had not paid attention to where we were. Our arrival had not gone unnoticed. I didn't understand what the harsh voice said but Gem whispered, "They ask who we are, Master."

"Thank you, my child. Tell him we are a poor monk and his guide and that we humbly ask for a shelter for the night."

Gem didn't get the chance to translate this, however. Out of the dark, two pair of hands seized us and we were dragged into the village. Soon we arrived at a central place, where a big fire was burning. There we could see our captors for the first time. They were two young, strong men with hard faces, in spite of the cold dressed only in short skirts.

Around the fire, many like them were sitting or milling around. They were all men—later I saw that women were kept separate, in the back. Our captors pushed us towards a big man with long black hair that flowed abundantly over his shoulders and with painted stripes on his face that seemed to glow in the light of the flames. He had a very grim expression on his face and his voice was loud and theatrical.

I swallowed. Of course God was with us—but I did feel a bit worried. The two men who had brought us here talked to the big man and Gem whispered translations to me until one of the men stopped her rudely.

I understood nevertheless that we were just in time for their yearly Great Offering to the Gods. The fire would play a central role in it—and so would we.

After a short exchange between the three men, we were thrown into a hut with a barricaded and guarded door.

Inside it was dark and foul-smelling. I couldn't see Gem, but I felt she was not afraid.

"Why do you feel so calm?" I asked, almost irritated.

She answered with great faith. "Because you are with me, Master."

I swallowed, and I was glad she couldn't see me. God is with me, God is with me, I repeated to myself again and again. But where was He?

I remembered the incident with the *vielfrass*. God had saved me there. He would save me again. At least, if that was His plan.

So I still felt worried. And worried was a bit of an understatement. My stomach seemed to turn around, my legs shook, I felt nauseous. I realized how much I wanted to rely on Gem now. Somehow, our many days together had given me the idea that she provided me with security. Had her company weakened me? When the *vielfrass* attacked me, I was calm. When I faced serious difficulties in the years before, I always felt the situation was part of *Maya*. Death, too, was part of *Maya*. Whatever would happen, it didn't matter. I never felt anything except calm, came good things or bad things.

I tried to breathe deeply to steady myself—silently, so as not to show my condition to Gem. Another uninvited feeling came to the foreground. Shame. What would Gem think if she understood how I was feeling? She would think I was not a monk; I was not the great person she always thought I was. She would surely not want to stay with me.

Suddenly this struck me as comical. It was a bit funny to worry about that, considering our short future.

I couldn't help myself. I started laughing. At first, it sounded a bit shaky—I couldn't remember the last time I had laughed—but soon there was more conviction in my voice. Gem heard my shaky laugh and asked, rather worriedly, "Are you all right, Master?"

At her question, my laughter increased. "Fine," I said, "just fine. Couldn't be better! And how are you today?"

After the laughter's initial strangeness had worn off, I felt a great relief. It was as if countless times emotions had been trying to come out through the door I always kept closed in order to be real monk. The tension in me had mounted and mounted. Now, finally, the door had given way.

I felt only now I had really come to life. The fact that this life would be very short I didn't mind. I lived now, here. What came after that didn't matter at all to me. The feeling of being alive sent waves of energy through my body. I felt totally centered and bubbling with joy.

"Master?" Gem asked. She seemed really worried now. To me, life was now the great game it was always supposed to be, God's *liila*. I felt an exhilaration, an unbridled joy.

"My dear Gem," I said, "We are leaving. I brought us in here—it's your turn to take us out. Let the drama unfold!"

She probably thought I had gone crazy.

I expected my Master to be unafraid. But how could he

be joyful?

But then, suddenly, I remembered something that he had told me some weeks ago. The world is an illusion; life is only a drama on a stage. At that time, my Master told me this very gravely. Now, in his great depth of spirit, he took it as something joyful, a drama to be enjoyed. His high-spirited mood was a deeply spiritual mood. Oh, to face death like that! I wished I could do that.

"Your turn," my Master said, almost teasing. He put his hands on my shoulders, shocking me for a moment, but then his touch removed my doubts. "Feel the energy of life flowing through you! With God on your side, you can overcome any obstacle in His drama!"

I did feel the energy flowing through me, joyfully, powerfully. It was a miracle.

At that moment, somebody opened the door. "What is all this noise?" a voice growled.

I started laughing. My Master started laughing again. From outside came confused voices over the crackling of the fire.

On the spur of the moment I said, surprising myself only afterwards, "We were talking with the spirit of my great-grandfather. He just told us what he was going to do to you all as soon as you harm one hair on our heads. Go ahead—it will be great fun!"

The words in the harsh dialect came to me easily. I heard the confusion outside increase.

Then a loud voice sounded, authoritative. It was the voice of the man with the paint and the long hair. He had heard us laugh, I think. He got a rapid explanation of what I had said. For a while he didn't say anything. Then he ordered us to be brought out.

A moment later, we found ourselves in front of him.

He towered over us, even over my Master. My laughter stopped. The man scowled at us and demanded, "What's that about your great-grandfather's spirit?" He bent down and brought his face close to mine. I smelled his stinking breath.

A spark of anger arose in me. "You are not going to bully me," I said under my breath. I felt the reassuring presence of my Master close behind me. The spark of anger turned into a flame. I wouldn't let him harm us.

"You ignorant lot!" I shouted to all the people gathered around the fire. A part of my mind looked on in stupefaction. I had never dared to say much in public, let alone shout. But I still felt the touch of my Master on my shoulders.

"The spirit of my great-grandfather is protecting us! He has saved us from bigger dangers than you! He'll curse your village! Everyone's hair will fall out, your animals will get sick, your crops will rot in the fields!" I felt an incredible energy flow through me. "You'll all die before the next winter comes!"

I almost believed it.

The villagers believed it completely. I looked around at scared faces.

"Go ahead!" I shouted. "Try to harm us!"

When I mentioned that their hair would fall out, I saw that the painted man brought his hand for a moment to his head, then dropped it quickly. After my last words, he looked me into the eyes for a long moment.

I stared back.

I saw how superstitious he was.

I refused to be afraid of him.

Finally, he took a step back. He turned to the two men who had brought us here.

He snapped an order I didn't understand, but they

cringed and quickly dropped on one knee.

Then they got up and came to us. Before we knew what happened, they took us away to the end of the village, from where we had come.

Behind us, I heard the painted man address the villagers, "The Gods were not satisfied with the sacrificial offering we were preparing..."

A few minutes later, we were alone again, under the full moon, unharmed. My Master seemed to have lost his incredible joy. He looked quite serious. Maybe he realized, like me, that we had been rescued miraculously. I, as well, became more my old self. But something in me had permanently changed, I knew.

My Master knew it, too. He looked at me in a way that was different from before. The light of the full moon was bright enough for me to see it clearly. His face reflected respect.

Winter, Second Moon, eleventh day

God rescued us from those barbaric villagers. I know that was the right way to see it. He brought us in that situation to learn something—Gem certainly did—and then He made sure we escaped unharmed.

But my pride sees it differently. My pride, my ego, tells me that Gem was the one who rescued us. Sure, I gave her the necessary push, because I was in that strange mood, but I feel I should have done more.

It should have been I, with superior power of mind, who faced the village chief and with just one look into his eyes made him cringe like a guilty boy and release us.

It should have been I, unruffled, with total calm and composure, who brought us out of the difficulties.

I feel embarrassed that it was Gem who rescued us. I feel even more ashamed of my initial fears.

Irrationally, I even feel angry with Gem for not becoming afraid, and not giving me the chance to be on top of the situation.

Dear God, why are you destroying my calm and self-confidence?

Winter, Second Moon, three hands' day

After our escape from the village, the days have been less blissful than before. My Master seems to be more closed, sometimes irritable. Of course, it can be that he does this to teach me something. I'm trying to find out what it is. Do I depend too much on his love?

Winter, Second Moon, eighteenth day

Gem hardly asks me spiritual questions anymore, and seems a bit afraid of me. It must be my dark mood.

When I realize this, I feel guilty. I should be grateful, and I should help her and be her guide on the spiritual path. Sulking is ridiculous. What kind of a monk am I?

I am a monk who isn't ready yet to be a monk, I admit with pain. I am no further than someone who has just been admitted to a monastery, to begin the long path towards self-mastery. And my teacher in this monastery—my teacher here is Gem.

Second Moon, four-hands' day

My Master started telling about spiritual things again! Although he does it in a different way now, I don't know how to describe it. But it makes me feel happy.

Today I dared to ask him a question again.

"Master, you told me once we should see God in the world. I was thinking, if the world is an expression of God and I am also an expression of God, then I don't have to feel afraid of anything. We are parts of the same. My leg doesn't have to be afraid of my hand. They belong to the same body. I don't have to be afraid of the cold water in the river. It can't harm me because actually we are part of the same."

My Master nodded. "That's very true, Gem."

"But Master, this morning when I had a bath in the river, I felt terribly cold. Why?"

My Master smiled. "You understood that you and the water are both a part of God. But did you truly feel it, this morning?"

I hesitated. "I thought about people who had drowned. Water can be dangerous."

He nodded again. "It's true. It's a matter of your awareness. As long as you feel the separation between you and the water, it is cold and it can even kill you. As soon as you feel one with it, it cannot harm you. I have seen other monks walking barefoot on glowing coal. They didn't feel anything. It didn't even make their feet black."

I thought deeply about this. "But suppose a *vielfrass* comes, and he wants to kill us. What would happen if we felt very deeply that we were an expression of God and he was an expression of God?"

My Master looked in the distance for a moment and seemed to frown. I suddenly wondered, what had he thought when the *vielfrass* was ready to attack him?

A faint smile broke through my Master's frown.

"Then God intervenes," he said.

I let that sink in. We didn't say anything for a while.

Then another, deeper thought struck me. "Master, what will happen if I do meditation and I feel very deeply that I am an expression of God and my meditation is an expression of God and the one I meditate on is God?"

"Then God will be doing your meditation, Gem."

He looked at me and said, "Can you imagine how deep that meditation will be?"

I tried for one moment and I had to sit down quickly. I felt overwhelmed by what I imagined. I closed my eyes. Without wanting it, I sank into deep meditation.

My Master told me afterwards that I had stayed in it for two hours. I don't remember much of what happened in that time, except that it was beautiful. All my fears, all my worries were gone. I felt so peaceful—I cannot describe it. I felt in perfect harmony with everything that exists.

Strange enough, the rest of the day my whole body was stiff. My Master taught me how to massage most of the discomfort out. We were close to a village and he got fresh milk for me and warmed it on a small fire. That day I started to cry many times without knowing why. But I felt very good every time. I felt that I let go of something that had bothered me for a long time.

For several days after this experience, I felt very peaceful. I hardly talked. All things I saw seemed to be in a quiet way beautiful. All things I did seemed to have that same quality. I felt God's presence in everything.

What Gem experienced, even I never experienced in fifteen years of meditation. She reached *samadhi*, a state of mind in which you experience oneness with everything. At that moment, you feel one with God.

I know about it; I saw it happen a few times in the monastery. People who are physically not prepared, feel stiff and painful afterwards—the energy that went through their bodies was too much for them to handle.

There must be a way to prevent this trouble. The only solution I know is fasting, to make the body less crude—but that is insufficient for most people. I heard that somewhere in the east they are using a system of physical exercises, postures actually, that make the body more subtle and the nervous system stronger. I wish I knew more about it. It would make the meditation easier for everyone, at every level.

Gem's *samadhi* caused a pang of jealousy in me; she experienced something that I had more right to than she. But the energy of her spiritual experience affected me, too. I felt unexplainably peaceful.

Winter, Second Moon, five-hands' day

For a few days the weather was almost warm.

We had crossed a savanna-like plain. At the end there was a forest. Just when we came near the first trees, clouds gathered all of a sudden above our heads. Before we knew what happened, rain came down in torrents. We found shelter under a pine tree, for a moment, but the water soon started to leak through the needles.

"That one over there is better!" my Master shouted over the drumming noise of the raindrops. We ran to the big tree he indicated, but halfway, he stopped to pick up branches from a tree that had fallen over recently. I stopped, too, and helped him collect more branches. Panting and wet we reached the big tree under which it was still dry. I laughed happily while I shook the raindrops out of my hair.

My Master had also lost his graveness. "We are going to build a palace," he said cheerfully. We worked quickly and efficiently. In a short time, we had made a crude structure with the branches and then we covered the roof with the twigs with closely packed needles.

Finally, my Master collected mud from around the tree, where the rain had not left one grain of sand dry, and we sealed the roof. We even managed to find enough small branches to fill up the sides of the hut, so that we had three good walls. The last open side gave us a good view of the still pouring rain.

"This should keep us dry for a while," my Master said, smiling merrily. We looked at our hands, mud-stained. I went to the door and stretched my hands out to the rain. In a few moments the mud was washed off. My Master followed my example. Then we withdrew into our tiny palace.

I told my Master about the hut I had built in the

tamarind tree and how I had weathered rainstorms there. I was suddenly open; I forgot my shyness. The running and fast working and our victory over the rain had made me excited. I felt that my eyes were shining, and my Master's eyes were shining too when he looked at me and seemed to drink in every word I said.

The next moment my mind suddenly seemed to grow. I didn't feel as if I were in my small body anymore, I was aware of much more. My body was still there, and I was still talking, but I was bigger than that.

I felt very free. I felt that my Master was not next to me; he was part of me, part of my big awareness. I didn't feel any boundary between him and me.

He, too, was aware of this. He had let go of his normal reservedness. We were together in this openness.

And in that big awareness that we shared, I felt God was there as well. I felt He was all around us and also with us; it was as if He had one divine arm around my Master's shoulders and another around mine.

The three of us were together.

A while later we continued our journey. My mind was still high. In some strange way, I could understand everything about myself and about my Master, too.

I saw our paths, intertwined; I saw our pasts and the things we had to learn in the future. I saw what my Master was struggling with at that moment.

I wanted so much to help him! But I felt that I shouldn't do that in my present role.

Later, later, I had to be patient.

A while later my mind came down to normal. I could not remember what I had understood about us. But I felt a deep love for my Master.

Winter, Second Moon, twenty-ninth day

The last few months I have been plagued by all kinds of feelings. A million times have I asked myself if Gem caused them and if I was a fool that I allowed her to stay with me.

I know it makes me more open to God. But it also makes me think less often about Him because my attention is nearly always on Gem.

Gem's company is temporary, I should remind myself. But I don't want to know this. Gem's love for me cannot be as deep and unconditional as God's, I should tell myself. But hers is so much easier to feel!

And I have this deep longing to take care of her, to make her happy. This longing is too strong to express. I should project this longing onto God. I should not have such strong feelings for a person. But how can I project this onto God? How can I make God happy?

The latest logic my mind came up with is that you cannot overcome attachment by avoiding it. Truly overcoming something attractive requires that you look it in the face and decide to let go of your longing for it. So I have to keep Gem with me now. Later I will decide to let her go.

Dear God, forgive me, but I hope "later" will be much later…

Winter, Third Moon, two-fingers' day

It is strange, with meditation. It lifts me up and I can see far and deep and understand many things. Then, afterwards, I feel a deep peace and happiness, but I am back on the ground and my old self again. I see my Master again as nearly perfect.

My old self again? Maybe in the way I talk and act. But deep inside of me there are new things.

Winter, Third Moon, fifth day

We arrived in a village called Freedom. They received us with curiosity and hospitality. During our meal by the fire (I noticed now what Gem probably had been doing for months already: she didn't eat anything of the meat she got and fed it secretly to the dogs that were always near) many of the men and the children surrounded us and asked us questions. Where did we come from, why did I have a beard, was I very old (because I was bald except for that thin ring of hair), was I Gem's father…

Gem tried to explain for the umpteenth time that I was a monk and we discovered again there was no word for monk in the local language. She patiently answered all other questions, sometimes with my help. I was content letting her answer what she could and just watching how she dealt with the questioners and enjoyed the attention she got. Now that she did meditation, her low moods were sometimes deeper but her good moods were even more beautiful than ever before. And the love she radiated…

She had confessed to me she felt so much love for everyone and everything, and didn't know how to express it. I thought her love was going in the first place to me, but painfully I discovered she meant what she said very literally.

She felt love for everything. Not more for me than for the villagers we met, for the dogs that jumped up against her and tried to lick her face whenever we came in a village, or for the trees on our path that struggled to survive the cold of the winter.

I found this universal love hard to accept. Was I not more special to her than others?

Of course, I didn't talk about this. But maybe she knew what I was feeling. "I can't help loving everything and everyone, Master," she said one day, "but of course some people are more special for me than others."

I reflected that I couldn't tell her what I felt, and she rarely told me about her feelings. Strange people we were.

I didn't know that soon I would ask myself a hundred times why I hadn't shown my love for her more openly…

The crowd around us grew and grew. Even the women came, shyly. The fact that Gem seemed to be my equal helped them to become more bold. Why were women always kept in the background, I wondered? Was it because in case of danger the men had to be in front to fight and protect them? But this had become a dogma and women were banned from most social events. It would be better if...

My reflections were interrupted. The whole crowd around us went through a perplexing change. Abruptly we had lost all their attention.

Nobody had walked away—but all had turned around. I saw only people's backs.

A moment later I understood the cause of this sudden change. It was visible over the heads of the people. I saw a rather young man, sitting high on something I couldn't see, riding past the gaping people. He had a mantle like I had, and an almost bald head like mine. He had to be a monk.

In all these years, only twice before I had met a fellow God-seeker. We had sat together in dignified silence, gravely appreciating the company of a like-minded person, but without any desire to exchange opinions about the weather or the hospitality of the villages where we had been. We didn't talk about anything. The next morning we had parted without more than a slight bow and we had never seen each other again. I didn't even know their names.

Our names are not important. We are not important. As God-seekers we know that only God is important. I haven't used my own name in years.

So here was another monk. But what was this monk doing so high in the air?

Then the crowd parted for a moment.

I stared. Gem gasped.

The man was sitting on a big black animal, sleek and noble as I had never seen before. It had slender but strong legs, dark mane, a tail made of hair and a narrow head that was simply beautiful. I was speechless.

The monk stopped. Everyone tried to come as close to the animal as they dared. The monk laughed—he *laughed*, I thought full of distaste—and bent down and lifted up a little boy who had been sitting on his father's shoulders.

He put the child in front of him on the animal. A shock went through the crowd. But the child laughed, full of glee, and the people relaxed.

Some men lifted up more children towards the animal, others gingerly touched it themselves.

"Hors," the monk said, patting his black companion on the flank.

"Hors," people echoed. From then on they addressed the man with "Hors" and he never corrected them.

Later, when the people had seen enough of the strange animal and found that it was difficult to communicate with the newcomer, they gave him food and showed him a place to sleep. All that time we had remained at a distance. However, I could see Gem burned with desire to speak to him.

I don't know why. I myself didn't have the least desire to talk with the man. What kind of monk rode so high and laughed so loud? I decided we would stay away from him.

But the man found us before I could do anything about it. He had the same undignified cheerfulness towards us as towards the villagers. I got the feeling he almost wanted to slap me on the back. He tried a few languages, grinning when we couldn't understand each other at first, and then we found the traders' language of the North that Gem and I used was for him not unknown.

With reluctance, I listened to the man. He declared without invitation that his name was Master Erdin, and he didn't seem to understand my disapproving silence when he asked for my name. It was bad enough that he gave away his name so carelessly. He should treasure for himself the name his Master had given him, and humbly remain anonymous towards all others.

And that he called himself "Master" was too much. Others may call a monk "Master", but not he himself. And even then the name has to be deserved. A Master is someone who has transcended all human weaknesses, who understands that the world is an illusion and who has seen God. I was given the name after a long and severe training, and— well, somehow my Master must have felt that I deserved it. It was not my decision.

This young monk, however, how did he get the title? Surely no Master would deem him worthy of it. Probably he himself had taken it, out of ignorant self-confidence.

When he found I didn't answer him, He asked Gem for her name. She beamed at him and said, "Gem, Master."

I didn't like this at all. This was the name *I* had given to her. She didn't need to share it with this young man. She could use her birth name. And "Master" was the name she had always used for me and nobody else. How could she call this man that?

The other brought us to the fire as if he owned it and talked to us non-stop. He babbled on enthusiastically about his travels and adventures in a way that suggested life was meant for having fun. Gem, blissfully unaware of my feelings, hung onto his words.

I withdrew in a haughty silence. From time to time I muttered to myself that this fellow was giving monks a bad name.

When the moon was at its highest point, I wrapped myself in my mantle and tried to sleep by the fire. Gem and the young man talked away most of the night, Gem eagerly supplying him with questions and exclamations. I'd rarely seen her so expressive. I didn't want to look at them, but I could very well imagine how she was looking at this "Master" Erdin. Her face would be radiant and her eyes beaming in her rapt attention for him. She looked that way to me when I talked about very serious and spiritual subjects.

This—this fellow, however, only laughed, grinned and chattered about trivial things he had done once upon a time. Why couldn't she hear the difference between insignificant and important things? Or actually, I admitted sheepishly to myself, why can't she see the difference between him and me?

When they finally went to sleep by the fire, I was still lying awake.

Winter, Third Moon, one-hand-and-one-finger's day

"Master, could you ask Master Erdin if he wants to travel with us for a while?"

I asked this to my Master the morning after I had heard all these wonderful adventures of Master Erdin. I couldn't bear the thought that he would leave us again. He was so nice, so joyful, so inspiring!

My Master didn't immediately answer. I saw now that he looked tired. Immediately I felt guilty—we must have been talking too loud last night when he tried to sleep. Finally, he broke his silence. "Monks usually travel alone."

I didn't understand. But of course I didn't insist. Maybe he would explain his answer later to me. I kept thinking about it, however. We traveled together. If my Master didn't mind that I was with him, how could he be disturbed by a spiritual person like Master Erdin?

Master Erdin had told me such beautiful things, I was sure my Master would like to hear them too. And he had told me about his help to many people, like the time when there was an epidemic and people suffered so much.

"Weren't you afraid that you would get sick too?" I asked him. He had shrugged and said, so simply, "They were all God's children...how could I let them suffer?" He has the same great love for people that my Master has.

I would like to help people, too. Together with my Master—wouldn't that be wonderful? I could do all the practical things, like feeding the people and washing them, and my Master would be there, giving his silent kindness that would cure the people so quickly.

When I was listening to Master Erdin, I was thinking of my Master at the same time and my heart seemed to burst with the love for them both. They are such great people. Oh, if only I could express my love for them. It's not normal love, like I had for my father. It's God's love—too big for my little heart.

Winter, Third Moon, sixth day

All right, I know, I shouldn't think anything bad about anybody. This so-called monk is also an expression of God. Even he. I mean, he too. But that doesn't mean he should spoil my Gem with his superficial chatter!

I can't stand it. What does she see in him? Doesn't she understand what is good and what isn't? I have to protect her. At the same time, I shouldn't say anything negative about other monks. But it's so easy, how he makes himself popular with Gem. I take the hard approach. Spiritual talk. Silence. Suffering. Later she will be grateful to me. But what has he given her?

Sullenly I put my few things in my bag. Where was Gem? It was time to leave this village.

At that moment she appeared. She looked torn. My anger was gone. "What is it, Gem?" I asked kindly.

She burst out in tears.

I waited until she managed to speak.

"Master, I don't know what to do. I mean I don't want to hurt you. I—Master Erdin, he asked me—"

It took a while until she had pulled herself together sufficiently to continue. "Master, he asked if—if…you know, he needs help with translating, too, and he would like if—if I could…

"Of course I know you can't be hurt, Master, but I still feel bad asking it…"

I felt nothing. Just a little cold spot in my stomach. I heard myself say, very calmly, "You want to go with him."

Gem looked anxious at me. "Er, yes Master… I told Master Erdin that I wished we could stay together, all three of us, but he said the same as you, monks don't travel together… And he said I needed different teachers to learn different things, is that true?"

I didn't answer and she continued, "Of course I will only go with him if you give me permission, Master…I'm sorry…I want to help you, too, but Master Erdin sounded very desperate when he talked to me and he is such a good person and I want to help him, too…"

I didn't feel frustrated at all. Not angry. Nothing. Just this growing cold spot in my stomach.

"You want to go with him," I said, again very calm. I turned around and picked up my bag. "Well, why don't you do it?"

I walked away without looking back. After a few moments I heard Gem call me, "Master?" She sounded puzzled. I didn't answer.

What does she understand of what she is doing to me? said an angry voice in me. I suppressed it with force. I kept walking. When I left the village, in the direction from where we had come the day before, I looked over my shoulder. She hadn't followed me.

Spring, First Moon, one-hand-and-four-fingers' day

I didn't know my Master would take it so easily. He was like I had seen him in the beginning: calm, detached—nothing could bring him out of balance. He just picked up his things and left. I wish I were so detached. I found it hard to leave him!

I have been traveling with Master Erdin and the horse for more than one moon cycle now. The horse's name is Hu, at least that's what Master Erdin calls him. Master Erdin is such a good person; he wants only me to sit on the horse; two is too heavy, he said. Sometimes we both walk, to give Hu a rest.

Master Erdin is always cheerful; he is fun to listen to. The distances between the villages never seem long. I feel light, happy. I realize now that my Master is so far developed and so deep and serious that it was often heavy for me to be with him. No, it is not that I didn't love him... It's just that I am such a beginner. Maybe the difference between us was too big. It is good to be away from him for a while.

For a while?

I thought about my own thoughts. Gem, I said to

myself, you will not meet him anymore.... He went to the north, you went to the south, you are many, many days apart—how can you ever find each other again?

But another part of my mind said no, we are not far away from each other. I always feel that he is still with me. I think about him in the day and I think about him every night before I fall asleep. Now I feel just love for him, not this painful feeling of having too much love. It's perfect like this.

Sometimes I talk to my Master, before I fall asleep—there are things I cannot tell Master Erdin. I understand better now how much I trust my Master.

Master Erdin doesn't meditate. I found that strange, at first, because he is a monk! But he said he talks to God. He calls it "praying". I don't understand how you can talk to a big, infinite Force. It's like an ant calling out to a mountain! But of course, Master Erdin knows more than I do.

We have been helping people, Master Erdin and I, just as I wanted to do! Master Erdin knows much about planting vegetables, especially about those that grow in winter. We came to several villages where people didn't know these things; they had only food in the summer months and even then not much because their land was dry and infertile. They were eating mainly meat from their cows and from the hunt and they were all sickly.

Master Erdin told them many things and showed them how to dig channels and bring water from a nearby river, and I translated. He also gave them seeds! He carries many seeds with him, especially winter vegetables and also something he calls soybeans. I'd never heard of them before. He says it is better than meat and good if you have no milk.

I discovered many things about my Master. I see in

Master Erdin things my Master also has, but never talked about. Feelings, wishes, and what Master Erdin calls imperfections. I always felt that my Master didn't want me to pay attention to that side of him.

Master Erdin doesn't mind that I see his imperfections; he even talks about them. He says many times that he is not perfect, and he doesn't feel guilty about it. Isn't that strange? But it is also nice for me. I am not perfect at all—and maybe that is not as bad as I thought.

Master Erdin sometimes gets angry with people, even scolds them if they treat us badly. I understand now that my Master was also angry with some villagers, but he never showed it.

Master Erdin tells me that sometimes there are many restless thoughts in his mind. He fights with him, he says. If I look at his face in these moments, I recognize that my Master was doing the same thing. He never told me. Maybe he was ashamed of these thoughts? That cannot be true. But he didn't want me to know about it. Maybe he was protecting me against things that were not good for me yet.

Anyway, I am so glad that I learn all this from Master Erdin. Now I know I am not the only one with many restless thoughts in my head!

Spring, First Moon, eleventh day

Master Erdin taught me to say "eleventh day", instead of "two-hands-and-one finger's day". Much faster, once I had practiced it for a while. I can count now without hands and fingers until ninety-nine!

When Master Erdin teaches me such daily things, I don't feel so different from him. He is also much more my age than my Master. I feel, in a way, closer to him than to my Master. Maybe I shouldn't feel that; I shouldn't feel close to a monk.

Spring, First Moon, twelfth day

Today I remembered the soothsayer again. And her strange words that I would live with two men. She had been right. And I am so happy! God takes care of every-thing. I wanted to live with the two Masters. And now I do. Master Erdin is here, and my Master is also here. He is in my mind and in my heart. I understand him better than before. I feel closer to him than ever before, now I know he has his shy side and his doubts and his other imperfections. Poor him, he always thought he had to behave to me as if he was perfect! That must have made him so tired...

Spring, First Moon, fourteenth day

I wonder what my Master is doing now. And if he sometimes remembers me. No, I think he doesn't. He may not be perfect, but he is a great monk. He lives in the present. When I was with him, he wanted me to stay; I understand that now. He was happy with the small things I could do for him. But now he has other things to think about. Monks don't carry their past with them, he told me once. His spirit is with me, I believe that. But his mind is free from attachments.

Spring, First Moon, fifteenth day

Sometimes I wonder how I can see that Master Erdin is a monk. He is not much older than I, he is not perfect, he is not grave, and he talks in a friendly way to women in the villages.

I don't mind, though. I like him as he is.

Spring, First Moon, sixteenth day

With my Master, I always did my best to behave very well, to make not a single mistake, to understand everything he explained. I always walked "on my toes", as they called it in my village.

With Master Erdin I feel more at ease. I don't have to do my best; I can be myself. I saw today how I even walk differently, more happily. I feel more free. Master Erdin is not really a Master; he is a friend. Isn't it wonderful?

He taught me tonight about the stars. We hadn't made a fire yet, and we were lying on our backs and looking at the sky. Master Erdin told me about the different constellations (it took a while before I could say that word without stumbling) and he knew stories about each one, great stories. Like the tale of the hunter who runs off with the princess, and the wizard who chases a goose through the sky, and the warrior who bears a torch and searches for the treasure at the other end of the world.

Oh, he tells stories so beautifully!

First Moon, eighteenth day

Master Erdin asked me to call him Erdin, without "Master". I was shocked. He is a monk. I have to respect him.

First Moon, nineteenth day

I felt silly, but I tried talking to God—praying, like Master Erdin does. I didn't hear any answer. Yet it was nice to talk like that. Erdin said God understands me completely, and loves me completely.

First Moon, twentieth day

I'm learning to brush Hu, the horse. He likes it when I take a forked branch and go through his hair, or when I rub his skin with dry grass wrapped around my hand.

Before I was a bit sad that Master Er—that Erdin was giving so much attention to Hu and sometimes seemed to forget me, but now I feel happy. We take care of Hu together.

First Moon, twenty-first day

It seems very natural now, to say "Erdin". I guess I just had to get used to it. We are not a teacher and a student anymore.

I talk a lot to him, about all kind of little things from my life in the past, or from my thoughts now, things that I always found too unimportant to tell my Master. I feel so light, so carefree. Often I want to sing!

First Moon, twenty-third day

I asked Erdin—with some fear—if it was right that we behaved like friends. I was afraid he would say a monk actually shouldn't act like that.

But he said, "You know, there are different kinds of monks. Some are monks on the outside, because that is good for them. Me, I am a monk on the inside. That's the most important thing."

I am not sure what that means. I didn't know there are different kinds of monks. But in any case he says it's all right what we are doing.

First Moon, twenty-fifth day

Erdin seems very happy that I am so happy with him. My heart makes little jumps when he looks at me.

First Moon, twenty-sixth day

I suddenly realized that I hadn't thought of my Master for a long time. It is as if my life with him happened many harvests ago. Do I miss him? I have to say I don't... My mind is too full with other things now.

First Moon, twenty-seventh day

It seems it has always been beautiful weather, the last week or so. Everything is beautiful. The trees are beautiful, the birds are beautiful, the sky is beautiful.

I stopped doing meditation a while ago. No need for it. And my heart dances all the time—my mind can't stand still anymore.

First Moon, twenty-eighth day

We were in a village where people had many questions for Erdin, and I was watching from a distance how he talked with all the people that had formed a circle around him.

Suddenly I heard a voice behind me. "Looking at him all the time, eh?"

I turned around, startled, and saw an old, old woman, her face all wrinkles and her eyes brown and shrewd.

"You are in love with him, aren't you?" She put a tiny dried-out hand on my arm.

"I love him," I said with dignity, and pulled my arm away. "Not in love."

The old woman chuckled. Her face softened. "Crazy love, then," she said. "But I know, it's part of your path. Don't worry."

I didn't like what she said. I wasn't worrying about anything.

My feelings for Erdin were wonderful.

First Moon, twenty-ninth day

Being with Erdin is joy when we talk; it is thrilling when he looks at me.

But it's tiring, too. My mind jumps, jitters, shivers, dances... I have no rest.

Spring, Second Moon, third day

We were in a village where we showed the people how to plant soybeans, and I helped Erdin digging holes in the ground at the right distance from each other. We were quite close to each other, and sometimes our hands would touch.

Every time that happened, I felt as if little flames went through my whole body. It was a scary and wonderful feeling at the same time.

When we were further away from each other again, I felt empty and I had a deep, deep longing to touch his hand once more.

I have no peace... Sometimes I wish all this would stop for a while.

Spring, Second Moon, fifth day

Erdin, Erdin... There is nothing else in my thoughts. I feel joy when he looks at me; I feel pain when he is away for a moment. I feel lonely when he talks to other women in the villages and seems to forget me. Oh, those are the most difficult moments of all.

Only in the night, when he sleeps at the other side of a village fire, I feel peaceful, because when I dream he is with me all the time.

But the next morning the longing, the pain, the joy that is too much to bear, they are all back. The joy is painful. It's always mixed with the fear of losing him.

This night I remembered my Master again, and I remembered how peaceful it was with him. Even when I was confused, or sad, or angry with myself, there was a kind of peace in me. I have never realized this before.

Spring, Second Moon, seventh day

I want to meditate and feel quiet, but I can't. All the time my thoughts and feelings keep on shaking me.

Instead of meditating, I talked again to God, this night. It helped a bit.

I began when I tried to sleep but I kept thinking about Erdin. I told God I want peace, and that with Erdin I never have it. I told God I want to meditate, and that with Erdin I can't do it anymore.

I should live alone, I said, and feel you again, God, but I can't give up Erdin. He is so gentle; I love his funny jokes; he is sometimes so boyish and sometimes so wise... He is open, honest... He is so helpful, and so faithful...and he is deeply spiritual.

He is everything I need.

Just—I feel no peace with him.

And inner peace, I said to God, harmony with myself and everything around me—that is what I want more than anything else.

Why can't I have Erdin *and* peace?

After I had said all this, I felt a bit better. But not peaceful. Sleep was far away. I turned from one side to another and back again.

"God," I asked silently, "please tell me what to do!"

There was no answer. The fire crackled, in the background village guards were talking softly. Everybody else seemed asleep.

"God," I asked again, deeply, intensely, "please tell me what to do. I can't go on like this."

There was no answer.

Why didn't God help me? I had asked so sincerely for his advice.

It was half a sleepless hour later that I suddenly realized that I didn't really ask God what I should do. I just asked: please, give me both peace and Erdin.

I thought about that for a while. Then I took a deep breath. I tried to accept the possibility of giving up peace.

No. Clearly that was not right.

I took another deep breath. Now I imagined leaving Erdin.

Aw, that was so painful. I felt so lost... What reason to live did I have without him?

Nevertheless I tried very hard to accept that possibility. It hurt, it hurt... But I kept trying.

"God," I asked for the third time, "what should I do?"

And all of a sudden, my eyes seemed to be opened. I realized that until now, something had held my thoughts in a strong grip, as if there had been an iron band around my mind. I could only see Erdin, Erdin, Erdin. Now, suddenly, I made contact with the rest of the world again. What a relief that was!

Close to me, I became aware of a little blackened branch that had fallen from the fire. I had seen it before, but now I really saw it. And I became aware of the blanket that covered me. I saw the silhouettes of the nearest huts of the village. I saw the dark dome of the night sky. I saw the stars—and at that moment I became aware of everything in the world.

My mind was free, no longer attached to anything or anyone. In that radiant moment, I saw—I felt—the stars, the earth, all people, animals and plants, all things. And I saw the Whole that they formed.

I saw God. God was all of them together. God was that Whole.

Maybe this feeling lasted only a moment. But it seemed to be without time.

Finally, my mind came down to a more normal state.

But still I saw that everything in the world was a part of God. The silhouettes of the nearest huts had taken on an unearthly beauty, seeing the shaggy dogs sleeping near the fire gave me a deep warm feeling, even the little branch on the ground seemed to be a wonderfully wrought treasure.

Everything was God.

Then I thought of Erdin, and of myself.

I saw what a silly girl I was, a silly but lovable little girl, so naive but with so many good intentions... And I saw Erdin, who was full of stormy, confusing thoughts, attached to his horse, addicted to having fun, feeling helpless without me...

It was strange to see this Erdin; he wasn't like I had thought before. I saw he was a very good man, too, helpful, honest and working hard to become mature. But not perfect at all.

I suddenly couldn't imagine how I had been bewitched to think all these silly thoughts about him, in the past weeks. It was nice to be with him, he taught me good things, but I could also live without him, if that was my life's path.

I felt deeply calm. All stormy thoughts and feelings of the past seemed faraway, unreal. There was no reason for them. I didn't need Erdin or anyone else.

Spring, Second Moon, eighth day

The next day, Erdin felt the change in me. I was very loving towards him—for the first time to him, not to the silly picture of him that I had had in my mind—but he clearly missed my "crazy love" for him. He was confused, he felt pained.

I felt sorry for him, but I didn't know what I could do to help him.

We stayed in the same village where we had slept that night. As always, many people asked Erdin for advice about all kinds of things, from growing vegetables to solving quarrels between villagers.

I had nothing to do and I talked with some of the women. They began to bring their children to me, some with questions, some because they felt the calm and centeredness in me. I felt happy in a peaceful way. I picked up the children and held them for a while, while I talked with the women about women's things. They trusted me. I didn't feel shy. The mood from last night was still with me.

The next night, before I went to sleep, I talked again with my Master, like before. I told him what had happened—in short, because I didn't want to bother him. But it was too beautiful to keep for myself. I didn't know if he heard me, but I felt good talking to him again.

Early the next morning I meditated for an hour.

It was in the afternoon that we left the village. We walked besides the horse for a while, silently, Erdin confused, I peaceful. What Hu thought, I didn't know.

It was cold, it even snowed for a short while, but I didn't feel it. I kept trying to make my mind bigger so that I would feel again that everything was one, was God. I found it I couldn't do it at that moment.

But I looked around me and said to myself, "The path is God, the snow is God, Erdin is God, I am God..." That already gave me a wonderful feeling. I felt we were all together; there were no boundaries between us.

It made me full of love for everything.

Spring, Second Moon, fifteenth day
Last night I couldn't sleep. I didn't know why. I told

myself that my sleeping was also God. Still, I remained wide awake.

Maybe I was not supposed to sleep, then.

I thought about the day, and I thought of my Master. This I did every night for a while, but something was different this time. I let God do the thinking.

I normally remembered my Master, imagined that he was there. I talked to him. This time, it came to my mind to wonder what my Master was doing now. I didn't think about it. I just—listened. I didn't imagine that he was here, like before, I imagined that I was with him.

And strange enough, I became very sad. I even cried, and crying I fell asleep.

Spring, Second Moon, seventeenth day

The next few nights it was the same. I sent my mind out to him and I became sad. He felt sad, I understood.

I began to remember things he had said and done and gradually I realized that he was, in fact, able to miss someone. Miss me, I should say.

When I was with him, he needed me. He depended on me. Not so much on my translations. He depended on my presence. When I put together all his words and looks and gestures that I remember, I saw it clearly.

Then, last night, I recalled all of a sudden—where had I hidden it before?—the last day with him and Erdin together. How he had withdrawn. How he had left abruptly.

Finally I understood. I felt terrible.

What had I done to him...

Spring, Second Moon, nineteenth day

I postponed it for two days.

But today I told Erdin that I had to leave.

It was difficult for me to say it. It was painful for him, and painful for me to see that.

I couldn't look at Erdin's face.

I said goodbye and walked away. A wave of sadness washed over me. I knew it wasn't mine.

I wanted to turn around, and run back to hug him and console him. I fought with myself and won—just. Yet I could hardly walk; my legs wanted to give way with every step I took forward.

I took a deep breath, trying to steady myself. "I am not he." I said to myself. "I am not sad—and I am doing what I feel is right."

That made me feel a bit stronger. I continued walking, without stumbling now. I sent a wave of warmth back to Erdin. I don't know if he felt it.

Why can't we all be happy? I exclaimed silently.

"That's the nature of this world," I heard my Master's voice in my head, from a lecture long ago.

But there had to be a way.

The Search

Am I a secluded figure?
In the Vast a little ameagre?
No, no, no, no, I am not alone
The Great is with me.

From Prabhat Samgiita – Songs of the new dawn
by Shrii Shrii Anandamurti

Spring, Third Moon, tenth day

When I set out to find my Master, I had no idea where he was. All I knew was that he had gone to the north while we went to the south.

In the beginning, I just followed the trail back to the village where we had separated. But soon I realized that this wouldn't help. My Master probably walked as fast or faster than I did. He was already one and a half moon cycles ahead of me. I would never catch up with him.

So I let myself be guided by my inner contact with him. I tried to feel inside of me where he was now, in which direction I should go.

That was not an easy solution. It meant I took the shortest route: off the beaten path, straight through uninhabited areas that took days to travel. I crossed dense forests, treacherous bogs and rivers without bridges. It was far worse than that very first day, when I was also in search of my Master. To make it even more difficult, I was going north now, and it became colder. Spring comes late here. And often I slept in the open.

Again I sprained my ankle; this time when I tried to go down a steep precipice and the stones under my feet started rolling. I rolled with them for twenty meters or more and I was lucky that I didn't break anything.

But I had to stop walking and for three days I had hardly anything to eat, since in the place where I was stuck, there were almost no plants. I became very weak. But that helped to make my mind silent and clear and my meditation was very deep. In that silent state of mind I thought three times I heard my Master's voice calling my name.

In that silent state of mind, I also remembered to see everything as an expression of God. The place where I was, my Master whom I wanted to find, the wish to find him, and finally, myself.

When I did this, my awareness changed. I saw how he, and I, and my wish to find him, were connected. I saw how we all fit in the Whole that the world is. And I could see what the direction was in which everything was going. I saw how the river was flowing towards the ocean.

At that moment, I understood how I could find my Master.

I ignored my ankle and my weakness and continued my journey, in the beginning hopping on one foot or simply crawling.

This high state of awareness slowly disappeared. But I kept repeating "everything is an expression of God", and for a while I felt the direction in which I had to go.

In the beginning, I remembered Erdin often, and I wondered how he was. I felt guilty. But when I felt part of the river of life, I suddenly understood. I saw how our time together and the end of it, had been part of the Flow of Things. It had been arranged exactly like this, to help me and to help him learn very valuable things.

I became aware, I somehow knew, that he understood more about himself now, and he understood better in which direction his path lay.

I felt at peace.

I walked many hours every day. I covered long distances. No tiredness, no hunger or thirst could stop me. I only thought of my goal. I came to villages where they didn't trust me—who was this girl who walked alone through the wilderness with torn clothes and wild hair and (as someone told me) with a fearsomely determined look on her face? Some people thought I was a witch and twice I was chased out of village by an angry mob.

I learned to approach mainly the women, when they were working in the fields. They were less aggressive to me than the men. I managed to get new clothes from a friendly girl and another one offered to cut my hair. Then I looked much better.

So much better, it seemed, that in the next village the chief noticed me and decided to marry me to his son.

When he saw I was not going to let him, several men helped him to bind my hands and feet, and they put me in a hut with a guard in front of it. The marriage would be after two days, when the moon was full. I bit their hands when they tried to feed me and I screamed at them. My Master would have said I grew a lot, those two days.

Then something very unexpected happened.

All this screaming and biting was good, but it didn't help me to free myself. In the second night I was lying awake, worrying. Suddenly, a shadow entered the hut. It didn't seem one of the people I had seen before.

I couldn't see the face, in the darkness. But with a shock I recognized the smell. It was the strange smell I had smelled so many moons ago, from the soothsayer in our village.

"Is that *you*?" I exclaimed.

"Hush!" the other whispered. She bent over me and I became sure. The same smell—but less sour than I remembered.

She pulled at the ropes that bound my hands and ankles. Then she took something from her belt, and with a snap, she cut the ropes.

I was too confused to ask questions. I rubbed my ankles and feet to get back the feeling in them. She beckoned me to follow her and we slipped out of the hut. In front of it, I saw a man lying on the ground, unconscious.

No one noticed us when we made our way to the edge of the village. There we stopped for a moment, because my feet didn't co-operate very much. We sat down. In the bright moonlight, we could see a forest not far away.

If we can get there, we can hide, I thought. I rubbed my feet as hard as I could to get the blood going. It felt like needles were stuck in one of them.

I looked at the soothsayer, and she looked at me. She looked cleaner, and younger; maybe as old as I was.

"You have changed..." we said at the same time.

Because of the tension of our escape, we started giggling like two young girls.

Quickly we stopped and listened. But no one seemed to have heard us.

"Why..." I started.

"I waited for you here," the woman said. "I didn't know that they would try to keep you here, but I knew you were coming."

"But why..." I began again.

"I just wanted to see you," she said. She looked at the ground.

I didn't understand.

"Are you still traveling around, scaring people?" I asked, thinking of the way she had talked to our chief and the other villagers.

"Sometimes," she said, not looking at me. "I try not to."

I believed her.

"Why are you here?" she asked me. "Why did you leave your village?"

It seemed she could only see bits and pieces of people's future.

"I am looking for my Master," I said. "He is a monk." I told her what he looked like. "Do you know if I will find him?"

She looked at my face for a long time. It seemed to me she saw many things. Finally she said, "Maybe."

"Why?" I asked. "Is the future not sure, then?"

She shook her head. "It depends on you."

Now we heard, from the center of the village, confused sounds and shouts.

"We have to go," she said, jumping to her feet.

We got up and started towards the forest, as fast as I could. There were many needles in one of my feet and the other foot was without feeling. I kept losing my balance. My rescuer helped me up more than once.

"What's your name?" I asked one of those times.

She looked at me for a moment. "Jamilla," she said. We started running again. She didn't ask my name.

Soon we were both getting out of breath.

I looked over my shoulder from time to time but I didn't see anyone yet.

"Why is the future not sure?" I panted after a while. It seemed more important than our escape.

"It depends...on our will..." Jamilla answered between quick breaths. "We make our future. God gives us chances...chances to learn things...What we do with them...depends on us."

When we reached the first trees, shouts behind us told us that they had seen us. We ran into the forest, and stopped after a while behind a big tree.

"So you believe in God," I said to her. A warm feeling spread in me.

"Yes..." she said. After a moment she added, "But I wonder if he still believes in me."

The forest was not very dense. The trees had few leaves and were far apart. They would easily see us in the moonlight. We kept going, struggling over fallen trees and through thick bushes. My feet made it hard for me to continue. Finally Jamilla said, pointing at another big tree in front of us, "Can you climb in there?"

I can climb trees with one hand and a toe, I thought. A few moments later, I was on a branch high above the ground. I could see the villagers enter the forest, a stone's throw away from us. They could see me, too, if they would look up. "Come," I told Jamilla, "quick!"

She shook her head. "I have to distract them." She looked up at me, hesitating. "Tell me—how can I become like you?"

I didn't know what to answer. My mind was empty. Then I heard myself say, "Remember that you are an expression of God."

Her face was passive for a moment, then it lit up. The next moment she ran off. She made sure that she was so noisy that the villagers heard her soon, and with shouts and exclamations they followed her.

She escaped easily. The villagers came back an hour later, muttering and cursing under their breaths. They didn't see me when they walked almost straight under the branch on which I was sitting. I had to do my best not to start giggling again.

I waited until sunrise but Jamilla didn't come back. I realized I had known that already when she left. But I had the clear feeling that in the future we would meet again.

The next days I crossed endless plains in the burning sun. Later I went through a snake-infested swamp. I hadn't found my Master yet. But I knew now it depended on my will.

I didn't sleep the two days that I was in the swamp; I was so afraid one of those scary creatures would attack me. When I had finally left that place and thought I was safe, I stepped on a snake and got bitten. I don't know how long I lay delirious.

Somehow I recovered. I was very thin and weak when I set out again. Was it really my own strength that helped me to get better after the snakebite? Many times on my journey, strange things happened; help came in unexplainable ways and when it was most needed.

I thought in the beginning often that it was my Master helping me. I could always feel him with me, waiting for me.

But I also felt that his mind was in turmoil. I didn't believe that in that state he was able to create all these miracles for me. The help came from higher.

In the time that I traveled with my Master, I had always experienced God as a force, an infinite cosmic presence that was pure love. With Master Erdin I got to know the idea that God was like a person, that I could talk to him. Now, I also felt that God was also following me on my journey and helping me when I couldn't do things alone.

I learned he cared for me.

Spring, a while later (I've lost count of the days)
Today I found myself unexpectedly near my own village.
I must have made something like a circle; I'd had no
idea.

Recognizing the area, I decided to make a slight
detour from my route and visit my village, just to have
a look. I still had poison from the snake in my blood, I
was weak and sometimes I vomited. I had not given
myself enough rest after the snake bit me. A day or so
without traveling would be good, I said to myself.

(A voice in my head gently tried to warn me, but I
didn't listen.)

I was welcomed warmly by my aunt and uncle who
had been my stepparents for so long, and by Hari, one
of my suitors, who hadn't forgotten me. I slept a lot; I
ate a lot of healthy food. I didn't stay one day, as I
planned, I stayed more than ten days.

After that time, I couldn't understand I had really
crossed the country alone for nearly a whole moon cycle.
Nor could I imagine that I would continue. I decided to
stay another few days to get stronger.

Instead I became weaker, mentally. After twenty
days, I was sure that I couldn't leave anymore. All these
dangers awaiting me. Searching for my Master who
could be anywhere. I hadn't felt him close to me since I
arrived in my village. He seemed far away—almost only
a memory.

The people in the village said I had been crazy to
leave them. They might be right. I began to feel that I
belonged to the village—for the first time in my life. It
might be the right place to stay. Maybe I was meant to
finish the spiritual part of my life now.

I saw a lot of Hari, these days. I found that he was
actually quite nice. There were no little flames in my

body when I was with him, and that was good. I wanted peace. People looked at us and started to think we were going to get married. I knew that if I didn't marry now, I would always be alone. I was already so old, more than twenty harvests. So I, too, started to think about Hari and marriage.

Marriage would be nice, would be peaceful. I would serve Hari the whole day and he would give me the security of a house and food. With a bit of luck we could be happy for many harvests.

* * *

Spring, first day

After I left Gem, or rather, after she left me, the first day was difficult. But then I felt calm, undisturbed. For the first time since—well, since I met her. I realized that my conscience had never forgiven me that I had allowed a girl to accompany me. And only now I realized how much turmoil it had created in my mind that I wanted to give her love and didn't know how to do it as a monk.

It was good that I was separated from Gem now. I should look for God.

Two days I maintained my inner balance. I wandered around, I didn't think of Gem.

Then small things started to remind me of her. I couldn't communicate very well with the villagers I met. I would collect some winterberries for myself or dig up roots and feel totally uninterested in eating them. I wanted to collect food for someone else, not just for myself. I forced myself to eat. But I ate very little, those days, those weeks.

I would open my eyes during meditation, feeling that I was alone. My thoughts would wander off.

When I became a monk, I knew that worldly goals were not fulfilling enough for me. Having children, being honored, having power or possessions—these things gave limited, temporary happiness. So I discarded these goals.

I told myself that my goal was God. But I didn't feel Him. In reality, I chose a negative goal: to ignore everything that I thought was not God. I became indifferent to the world, to people, to myself. I discarded all my feelings, my wishes, my spontaneity. They didn't befit a monk. I knew better than being influenced by *Maya*.

From then on I felt peaceful. Or rather, I felt nothing. That lack of feelings I called peace.

Spring, twelfth day

My meditation is totally uninspired.

After nearly two moons without Gem, I realize I was too early with detaching myself from everything.

And all those feelings that Gem has "caused", are still here. She broke the dam that I used to hold back my feelings. I saw in her how I secretly wanted to be. Open, expressive. Trusting. Positive and loving to others.

I know now that I wanted to learn this from her. But it's too late.

Spring, seventeenth day

It's cold here. I'm tempted to use the heat mantra again. If I do it, I forsake what I learned from Gem.

Spring, eighteenth day

Today, at the beginning of my meditation, I remembered who I was before I became a monk.

I suddenly saw in my mind a picture of a small village boy, running full of enthusiasm over a rocky beach with a big, beautiful shell in his hands.

I saw an older boy, feeding a crippled deer that came to him daily from the forest.

I saw a young teenager shouting furiously at his father who had refused him permission to go for a hike.

I saw a sixteen-year-old in tears, looking at the girl he was in love with, marrying another man.

And I saw the three friends I had before I went to the monastery. We used to have countless deep-into-the-night conversations about Life. They were older than I, and most of the time they spoke. I listened breathlessly to their wisdom. Each of them had had his share of disappointments in his life, and they convinced each other more and more strongly that God was the only worthwhile goal. It was a difficult goal, they said, because God was far away and difficult to approach, but He wanted us to come to him.

Later one of my friends fell in love and married, and it turned out to be a disaster. One of the others tried to escape from seeking God by undertaking long journeys to exciting, far away countries. One day we got word that from his last journey he would not return.

I didn't dare to say it out loud, but I felt attracted to both things—marriage and traveling. My intellect, however, told me I was young and foolish. I had to search for God, it insisted.

Was that my own idea? Or had it come from my friends?

God certainly attracted me. But I kept thinking that there must be beautiful things in the world, too. I'd never been to the mountains or to the big cities. I thought it would be exciting to meet new and strange people, who lived in countries far away. And I kept thinking there must be a wonderful companion for me, somewhere in the world, with whom I could share all these things.

But the failed marriage of my first friend shocked me. And the death of my second friend made me sometimes wonder if that had not be his punishment for neglecting God.

I was young, I had foolish thoughts. Only now I know that God doesn't punish.

Then my third friend, to whom I had always been closest, announced he had had a dream, in which a voice from the sky invited him live in a monastery. He was so impressed by this that immediately he began to give away his possessions and embarked on severing all his ties with the world.

I watched him with a bit of jealousy. I didn't know how it would be to live like a monk, but at least my friend had taken a decision.

A few days later, he got afraid. He didn't want to leave all familiar things and people behind. He talked a lot to me and tried to convince me to come with him. I thought of the endless discussions with our little group and the fact that we didn't do anything with all that talk. I thought of marriage and of a failed marriage; I thought of traveling and I thought of God's punishment.

It all pointed in one direction.

In the end, my friend didn't take the big step. He got too scared. But I did. A few days after my twentieth birthday, I entered a monastery.

I felt I was leaving all foolish wishes behind. I was going to grow up.

Spring, nineteenth day

I found it gave me a feeling of peace, thinking about my past and seeing the path that had led me here. As a monk I never thought of my past before. The past was dead. A monk's life starts when he enters the monastery.

Thinking more about my past gave me another realization. I had chosen the path to God with the wrong motivation, but in hindsight, it had not been the wrong path. What would have happened if I had not gone to the monastery?

I would probably have married, sooner or later. Now to have a family is not wrong in itself. Marriage is fine for those who have a desire for a regular life with a partner and children, helped by God in the background.

But if you want God filling every moment of your life, if you want to feel all of God's wonderful consciousness, then you need to find him more important than your partner.

This is hard. In a marriage it's easy to get attached to your partner and make God less important. It happened to me with Gem, for a while. It would have happened to me in a marriage—forever, maybe.

So I'm glad I became a monk. I haven't felt yet how loving and wonderful God is, but I know I am on my way.

At least—I was on my way, when Gem was with me.

Spring, twenty-second day

The cold is gone.

It's spring. Trees have green fingertips.

The time with Gem helped me to realize that I don't have to concentrate only on God. I can concentrate on whatever I want as well. It will all lead me to God.

Gem was my most direct reminder of God. I feel pain whenever I think of God and realize that Gem is not here.

I should try to find her again.

I almost laugh. What an impossible idea.

Spring, twenty-fifth day

This morning I interrupted my meditation to watch the dawn. Majestically the sun rose. The sky became alive with colors; warmth began to fill the air. Shyly a bird started to sing. One very bright star remained visible for a long time, until finally the sun's radiance won.

I drank it all in.

Spring, twenty-sixth day

Sages say the sun is so far away that it would take many lifetimes to walk even halfway. And the stars—the stars are so remote that even the fastest bird with a thousand lives could not get there.

We can see a myriad of stars when we gaze up at the night sky. And there are many more, they say. There are more stars than there are water drops in a river.

Numbers and distances beyond comprehension.

And bigger than the sun, bigger than the space between us and the stars, is God.

Thank you, God, for reminding me of You every day and every night.

…I wish I could tell Gem about this.

Spring, Second Moon, eleventh day

I am a fool if I give up God's gift to me. I want to start looking for Gem again.

This morning, in my meditation, I felt a strong resolve to find her.

Spring, Second Moon, twelfth day

But today it seems pointless to have much hope. We are so far away from each other. Yet—I am traveling to the south again. To increase my chances a bit.

I want to ask in every village if Gem has been there. But people would look at me suspiciously. Why do I want to find a girl?

I make up a story about a family in another village whose daughter disappeared. I describe Gem and ask around if someone has seen her.

No one.

Spring, Third Moon, second day

Many a night I lie sleepless. I think of cold winter nights when Gem and I shared the duty of keeping the fire alive. She slept by my side, neither of us thinking about being man or woman. We were simply two human beings who gave each other warmth and protection, close in the experiences we had shared and in our common goal of life.

Spring, Third Moon, seventh day

I am convinced that there is nothing wrong with my wanting to travel with Gem. I don't care anymore what others might think.

I have begun to ask villagers outright if they have seen my former companion.

Spring, Third Moon, ninth day

I had walked the whole day without reaching a new village. The pale sun had set; it was getting dark. The temperature dropped quickly. I had to look around for firewood. I considered continuing walking, just to save me the trouble of making and maintaining a fire, but I felt that I didn't have the strength to walk a whole night.

Half an hour later I sat by a small fire. Maybe it wouldn't burn until sunrise, but I couldn't be bothered now. Tiredly I poked into the flames.

Suddenly, out of nowhere a thought came to my mind. "No, Gem, you shouldn't get married. It would be a prison for you. No, don't..."

It was as if I had to convince her. Why was this in my mind? We had never talked about it.

"Gem, you are one of the few people in the world who deeply long for God. You still have the freedom to devote your life to Him. Do you really want to give that up and get into that prison they call marriage?"

I felt she was not convinced. She thought she could get self-realization when she was married. And she was tired, so tired of wandering. She wanted a safe place, a house she could call her own. There she could meditate and find God.

"No, Gem... *Think*. Marriage means you're going to serve your husband, not God. You'll be working all the time, cooking for him, cleaning after him, taking care of the children, working in the field, keeping the fire going... When will you find time to meditate, to find God?"

I didn't know why I was saying all this. The loneliness was affecting me, I thought gloomily. I poked into the fire for a while. I nodded off. I woke up and added some wood to the fire. I nodded off again.

I wasn't sure, afterwards, whether the next thing happened when I had been awake or when I slept. All I knew was that I felt Gem sitting beside me, wearing the colorful mantle she always wore. It had been a gift from a friendly woman in some village on our way, I remembered. I could see Gem beside me. It was more real than imagination.

"Master," I heard her voice, filled with devotion. I could almost hear it with my ears. "I want to stay with you always."

I sat very still for a moment. I swallowed. She appreciated me so much. She gave me the love I couldn't give myself.

I deeply wanted to be with her again.

I was even willing to show her my real, imperfect nature.

Spring, Third Moon, sixteenth day

I don't get any help from villagers. Sometimes they are even hostile when I tell I'm looking for Gem. In one case, I had to run for my life.

Spring, Third Moon, eighteenth day

I struggle with severe opposition inside of me. I often hear a voice telling me how foolish I am. It seems to be my guru speaking. I have to listen to him.

Or is it my inner judge? The voice that judges me and so many of the people I meet, and drove me forth on a path that may not be mine? *Of course it's your path*, the voice that I ascribe to my guru says. *All other paths are foolishness.*

I notice how this voice keeps repeating itself. It doesn't seem to have many arguments. On the other hand, it must be right. My present behavior is just a temporary blindness, a short period in which I get pulled off the spiritual path by Maya. Monks have always known that Maya is doing this. Only the guru can save one in these moments. And yet. Something in me feels that there is something wrong. It has no rational arguments; it just feels terribly locked up in a tiny prison and struggles to get free.

During these inner fights, I find myself walking fiercely, nearly stamping on the ground, my eyes only seeing my sandals and the dust I kick up on the road. In my head, the storm rages on and on.

Spring, Third Moon, twenty-first day

I avoid villages these days. I feel I completely lost my ability to look grave and calm. It is spring, but at night it is cold outside. Fortunately, in the daytime, my walking and my struggle keep me warm enough.

I'm totally going off the path that was meant for me. Every monk has to go through tests; this is mine. I have to give up Gem.

Sometimes I see that quite clearly. Yesterday I changed my course and started walking back to the north again. My inner turmoil changed; my guru's voice—if it was his—disappeared.

But something else became stronger. I still had no peace. I

discovered at the end of the day that the sun was setting on my right hand side. My head follows my guru; my feet have a guide of their own.

Spring, Third Moon, twenty-second day
It is possible to ignore the voice in me that berates me for going south, towards Gem. But the constant struggle is exhausting. I don't know how long I can keep this up.

Spring, Third Moon, twenty-fourth day
To suppress the criticizing voice I started eating anything edible I found on the road, which I have never done before. It gives me a very unpleasant, heavy feeling. There's constantly a knot in my belly and also a fog in my head. It makes it hard to think clearly. In that sense, it serves its purpose. But I feel like an animal instead of a human being.

Spring, Third Moon, twenty-sixth day
Meditating is also not possible with a full stomach. I'm very restless, and during my night meditation I keep falling asleep.

For the rest I hardly sleep and I walk longer hours than ever, to digest the food and to escape the thoughts.

I cannot go on much longer like this.

Spring, Third Moon, twenty-eighth day
I'm exhausted from too much walking, too little meditating and too much struggle. I reached an end point today. I went off the road to do meditation, but instead of sitting in lotus posture, I just lay down on my back. I surrendered to the tiredness and the confusion. I stopped suppressing the voice in me. Immediately my inner critic sounded loudly. See what all this foolishness is doing to you? Turn your back on her! But this time I recognized it was not my guru's voice. My guru had been strict but loving. This voice was strict and nothing else; it was my inner judge. I let it shout and paid no attention to it.

After a while it came up less frequently. Finally, after a long time, it receded in the distance. I took a deep breath. I smiled feebly. My mind remained silent. There was no new voice to take its place.

My head had become still. It was like a muddy pond that became clear after the mud had sunk to the bottom. For the first time in weeks I could see further than Gem and further than the spiritual path I *had* to follow. I saw I was not the monk I was supposed to be. I saw I didn't need to walk the path that I thought was meant for me. I was unique; I had to find my own path in life.

And also I saw clearly that I was on the way to God.

I couldn't see very far, but this was far enough. Finally, I got up with peace in my heart. I kept my feet directed to the south without any comments in my head.

Spring, Third Moon, twenty-ninth day

Most people still don't want to answer my inquiries about Gem. But today I spoke with a woman working in a field. She told me about a village one or two days' walking away, where her sister had married just now; there lived a girl who looked like Gem.

But lived there? That can't be her.

* * *

Summer, First Moon, second day

This morning I woke up early. I was filled with a restless feeling. There was something on my mind but I didn't dare to face it.

I bathed in the ice-cold water of the river, returned shivering to my hut and nevertheless I felt warm. I considered for a short moment to do meditation, but I knew Hari would be coming and he didn't like seeing me do it. It had scared him the first time. "Gem, Gem," he had exclaimed anxiously, "it is as if you are dead!"

I ate some of the carrots that were left over from last night. I took the reed broom and swept the hut clean. I wanted to put more wood on the fire but I hesitated and for some reason decided against it. I collected the rest of the carrots and put them in a bag, together with a small clay bottle. I picked up my blanket, rolled it up tightly and stuffed it in the bag as well.

At the other side of the village, a cock crowed. It was dawn. Hari would come soon, to accompany me to his father's hut where we would have breakfast together... But I had eaten already. And why had I packed food and my blanket?

Finally it got through to me what had been in my mind since I woke up.

When the cock crowed for the second time, I had left the last huts of the village already behind me. My Master needed me.

Summer, First Moon, first day

When I walk, I constantly see Gem's face before me. I don't know where I am going to, I just follow her face. Most of the time there are no thoughts in my mind at all.

Today I walked the whole day. The surroundings looked familiar; maybe I had been here before. It didn't matter. At night, I wanted to meditate and rest but something kept me walking the whole night until I reached a village early in the morning. The sun rose hesitantly, a cock crowed twice. Maybe I could rest here for a while.

I looked around for someone to talk to. The first person I met in the village was a handsome young man, calling something between the huts. I was tired after a night without sleep, but I woke up with a start when I heard what he was calling. It was Gem's name.

For a moment I thought it was Hari who had come after me. Then—I could never forget the sound that I had heard so often—I recognized the footsteps. Although they were much faster than usual.

I don't remember what we said that first moment. I

only remember that I felt so many tears in my throat that I swallowed and swallowed to stem the tide. But it was too much to stop. I let the dam burst.

The next moment I remember, I clung tightly to my Master, crying and crying in his dusty mantle. He is taller than I am; I pressed my face against his chest. I cried without shame, without holding back. I cried out loud. I remember my Master's arms soothingly around me, his hands on my back. We stood there forever.

I remember how he finally disentangled himself, holding me at arm's length. He didn't say anything. He just looked at me. Then again, I remember my face pressed against his mantle. I had my eyes closed; all I experienced was the feeling of his chest against my face, his irregular breathing.

It seemed an eternity later that we separated again. My Master cleared his throat, coughed some more.

"The dust on this road is not good for us," he said. "Let us go."

The first few meters I walked a bit behind him, like before. Then I changed my mind. It was not right anymore. I quickened my step and began to walk beside him.

Companion

"You have found it in yourself," my Master said.
"It's the divinity in you. Your connection with God."

Second Autumn

It was maybe twelve moons after I joined my Master on his wanderings that he asked me one evening why I had chosen to follow him.

I thought for a while and looked at the stars that shone above us all over the sky. My Master added some wood to the fire.

At first, I was simply attracted by him as a person. His inner balance, his kindness. I must have guessed there were more qualities that were not visible yet.

But that doesn't explain why I left everything and ran after him, braving the cold, the wild river, the *meandi* and the *vielfrass*, without any certainty that I would find him.

"I think I followed you, Master," I said slowly, "because I felt not complete without you."

My Master raised his eyebrows, a habit he had gotten only recently. His face had become more and more lively, in the time I traveled with him.

"What were you doing before I came?" he asked. He had never asked me this, or any other personal question in all those twelve moons that we had been together. Yet I always felt he was very much interested in me, concerned about me. He loved me. I had slowly discovered that he was also attached to me.

Only recently, I realized how much trouble his feelings for me are giving him. His love is usually slightly withheld, or, when it sometimes gushes forth from him, it is tinged with doubt or guilt. I wish I could help him— but of course this is a part of his personal growth.

"I lost my parents when I was eight and fourteen," I said. I told him about my life until he had come. About the questions I had about where we came from and why we were living.

"I felt incomplete; there was something very special that I needed," I finished. "In the village there was nobody who could help me with it. Maybe my father could have given it to me. When he talked about God, I felt that was what I was looking for, young as I was. But my father died—"

I stopped.

"Have you found it now?" my Master asked.

I tried to meet his eyes, but he seldom looked directly at me.

"I have found it," I said finally. "In you."

My Master shook his head. "No," he answered. "Not in me."

I blinked. "Not in you?"

"You have found it in yourself," my Master said. "It's the divinity in you. Your connection with God."

He paused. "I happened to be the person who helped you to discover it. But it was all the time already present in you. You didn't believe that there could be something good in you, that's why you didn't see it at first."

I sat very still and let this sink in. I had always felt so good with my Master. I thought it was him.

He guessed my thoughts. "I'm just helping you to keep your door to God open. Soon you'll be doing it yourself."

I felt warmth spreading inside of me, hearing my Master's confidence in me. I smiled, enjoyed the feeling without speaking. I added some more wood to the fire.

Later I asked my Master, "Why did you accept me as your student?"

"Not student," my Master corrected me. "Companion."

My warm feeling deepened.

"But I learned so much from you, Master."

He seemed not to have heard me.

"Source of inspiration," he said.

Six moons ago I would have refused to listen to this. Now I didn't protest. I knew I wasn't his equal, but—yes. We were helping each other.

"I learned from you," my Master said gravely. "You asked me why I accepted you. Well, I needed you." He nodded slowly, seriously. "I didn't see it immediately when you came. But later I understood. We are fellow travelers on the way to self-realization."

His eyes got a faraway look. "You learned to see your inner strength and resources, and your divinity. You are ready now for the last part of your spiritual journey.

I learned to see the unfinished parts of myself, parts I had prematurely abandoned. Now I can deal with them and overcome them—and continue my path to God."

He thoughtfully poked into the fire with a long stick.

"We just have to continue on our path. When we accept ourselves fully, the road to God is short," he said. "It's not only our weaknesses that are in the way. It's the lack of love for ourselves. Without love for ourselves, we are closed, closed to God as well."

I looked at the ground. But not so long. I knew I was going in the right direction.

"How long will you stay with me?" my Master asked suddenly.

I smiled at him. Words came spontaneously. "Maybe our ways will part after some time. But not our hearts."

My Master looked as if he wanted to object. Surely, I thought, he wants to say that this would be a bondage, an obstacle on the spiritual path towards self-realization.

But he smiled also.

"That's good for now," he said.

Only a few minutes later I understood that he consciously did not voice the purely spiritual view. He realized that now he needed to concentrate on living with people. And on all the feelings that this brought out in him: love, irritation, jealousy, shame, attachment. And pain.

He was brave.

I shook my head when I thought of one harvest ago. Now I understood so much. Then I was naive, thinking my Master was perfect. I hardly saw a glimpse of all that went on in his mind and heart. Where had this young girl gone so quickly?

"Let's do meditation," I said to my Master. My companion.

I added wood to the fire. We closed our eyes.

Epilogue

I looked at the little girl in myself and smiled.
I learned to love her and her imperfections,
with all my heart.
- Gem

One night I suddenly woke up. That was not unusual; at sixty harvests, I slept lightly. But this time I woke up because I had received a message in my sleep. My Master wanted me to come. The message came as a shock. I suddenly felt very empty. My Master had died.

His wish was clear. Attending his cremation would be against his living rules and my living rules, but I didn't hesitate.

I left the ashram that I headed in the hands of one of the sisters, without giving her or anyone else an explanation. This was something between my Master and me.

I had to travel for two days to reach the place. The journey was tiring and at times dangerous. But the only thing I cared for was that my teacher had asked me to come. For what, though?

My arrival at the cremation created some whispers and raised eyebrows amongst the monks there. Who was this old woman?

But the eldest monk, my Master's successor, welcomed me without hesitation. He must have had instructions from my Master.

After the cremation, he led me to a small room. Until then he had not shown any doubt about my presence or my role in my Master's life, but now he seemed to have reached the limits of what he could accept. With great reluctance, he showed me into the room that had a stone bed as its only furniture. In the corner, there was a water jug. On the bed were three things. I recognized two of them immediately.

"He left something for you," the monk said with ill-concealed disapproval. "He must have felt they were his own."

I understood that in this ashram, no one had any possessions, and that when a monk died, the things he had used, went to anyone who needed it.

Gingerly, hiding a smile, I took the things one by one in my hands. The first was an old, battered clay jar with a big crack from bottom to top. I recognized it immediately as the one in which my Master had made tea for me that first night, when I had rescued him from a *vielfrass*, the most dangerous predator of that area. The day after that, the jar had gotten that crack and started leaking. I never thought my Master had kept it with him.

The second thing was his mantle that had kept me warm so many nights before I got one for myself.

The third—it took me a moment to realize what it was. It seemed a bunch of pale brown strings, each hair-thin.

Hair...

When we twice ran into trouble because villagers didn't accept a monk accompanied by a girl, I sacrificed my long black hair. My Master cut it off carefully and I always thought he threw it away. He surely didn't have any attachment to something "outer" like this.

I discovered I had been holding my breath since I picked up the last of the three things my Master had left for me.

Slowly I breathed out. Here were the symbols of the secret that we had shared: the period in his monk's life when he had taken the courageous decision to drop his facade and face his very human weaknesses.

I think it took him five or six harvests to overcome all of them. I was always with him in that time. Although he kept most of his struggles for himself, I could often feel clearly enough what he was going through.

I, too, went through much personal and spiritual growth and it was not always easy.

We wandered through the lands, stopping a few days whenever we saw we could help people. My Master gave spiritual lectures to those who were interested, which sometimes exhausted him but he never wanted to stop; I took care of sick people and told the things I had learned from Master Erdin about food. Once we got involved in a fight between two villages and my Master stopped them at the risk of his own life.

So many things happened to us. And we discovered many things inside of ourselves, some very good and others that needed letting go. I may tell about all our inner and outer adventures at a future time.

Let me just say that finally my Master became a monk with real graveness and real detachment from *Maya*. His graveness never prevented him from smiling every now and then. He even developed a subtle sense of humor that came out at unexpected moments. And I felt that behind his serious face he always smiled at people, at animals, at the whole world. And at himself... accepting his last remaining imperfections, his humanness.

Our time together helped me much. After six harvests, I had lost most of my unnecessary humbleness, and I had got more inner balance.

And yes, the questions I'd had since my childhood, got answered. My Master taught me higher techniques of meditation, and then I understood who made the universe, and why we are here on earth.

Often, everything that happened to me, all the things and people I saw around me—they all seemed right, in an indescribable way. Because I felt everything was part of the Whole. All things were an expression of God.

I found such a beauty in the creation. I wish I could give this realization to others. I tried many times to put it into words, to help people who had lost their hope in life; but spiritual experiences cannot be expressed in a spoken language. They can only come to you if you do meditation.

God became an inseparable part of our lives. I think my Master related to God in a more personal way than I do, but I didn't feel that as a shortcoming in myself. Everyone has his own way of experiencing God.

* * *

After those five or six harvests, I felt that my Master had overcome all his weaknesses. He had finished his learning period with me.

There was more that I could learn from him, but I felt it was time to go.

Out of a humbleness that was real, now, I got up one morning before he did and left silently.

He agreed. When I had been on my way for half an hour, it was suddenly as if I saw my Master in front of me. It was just one moment. He seemed to look at me, and gave me a simple nod.

Then he disappeared again. But I still felt his presence. Warmth spread through my whole body. In my mind, I felt, rather than saw, my Master's smile.

With this, a new part of my life started. For many

harvests, I wandered through the countries as a female renunciate, without ever meeting my Master again. I did meet Jamilla—but that's a story in itself. I often went through hardships and several times through dangers, and each time I would literally feel God's hand on my shoulder.

Most important, more than surviving the dangers, was that God's love finally convinced me to love myself. I accepted myself as a human being, and human beings have shortcomings and weak spots. I tried to overcome them, for sure, but I accepted myself as I was. I stopped condemning myself. I looked from a higher point of view at the little girl in myself and smiled. I learned to love her and her imperfections, with all my heart.

After twelve harvests, I arrived at a spiritual community for female renunciates. I had often seen the place in visions; I felt I was coming home.

The sisters welcomed me with more respect than I felt comfortable with. "I'm only a beginner," I protested often.

They wouldn't listen. They sought my company, they asked my advice. They gave me more and more responsibilities in the ashram. Two or three harvests later, the community's Mother passed away and I was to become the new leader of the sisters.

I had said, so long ago, that my Master and my ways would separate but not our hearts. I know now that our hearts did separate. A fully realized, detached person has no emotional connections with anyone in particular; he loves all equally. But at the same time, if he has shared so much and such a special part of his life with someone, he doesn't forget that person.

I knew my Master didn't forget me. As the Mother of the ashram, I was sometimes troubled by inner turmoil and I doubted that I had enough qualities to lead the sisters through our personal and material crises. But then, when even God within me didn't seem to respond, I felt a loving, soothing presence around me. Sometimes it was as if an invisible hand took my face, very gently, and lifted it up to the light that seemed at these moments brighter than before. My cheeks would flush like a young girl's and a feeling of peace would come over me. I always managed to solve the difficulties after that.

In the last fifteen harvests as the head of the ashram, I hadn't felt my Master's presence. The sisters considered me a spiritual Master myself, and truly I felt confident enough to guide them through mental and spiritual problems. The feeling of divine love that I had experienced in my very first meditation, had become permanently lodged in my mind. I knew everything was God. Still, there were moments that I felt I was only the student of my Master. It was probably my last weakness that I never wanted to acknowledge the title of spiritual Master that the sisters gave me.

Now, standing at the bed of my former Master, and looking at the things he had left me, I suddenly understood they were not signs of his attachment to me. Nor had he supposed that I felt attachment to these things.

He surely felt attached to me when we traveled together. After that, he must have kept these things as a reminder of a weakness that he had overcome. And with the sense of humor that he had developed in our last months together—the last step towards real monkhood, I had called it then—he had left me these things that only he and I could fully appreciate.

Leaving them here for me was like a glance of understanding between him and me. It was like saying, "See—

we needed this once and now we have overcome it. We are no longer bound by *Maya*."

I suddenly felt clearly how this was an expression of my Master's sense of humor. It was a very subtle smile. A message that could only be understood by equals. Equals.

I thanked the monk who had shown me the things and left them with him. He tried not to look puzzled.

When I left my Master's ashram and returned to mine, I realized that now I was ready to lead the sisters without any unnecessary humbleness. I was not my Master's student anymore.

My Master had given me his last guidance: he considered me a spiritual Master, too.

About the Author

Joost Boekhoven started writing when he was six, and he never stopped.

After high school, he studied physics for a few years, trying to understand the secrets of Life, then followed his musical inclinations and studied at the Rotterdam conservatory to become a pianist.

When Joost Boekhoven was twenty-five, he finished his musical studies and went back to his search for a deeper meaning of Life. He began to study yoga and meditation and practiced them daily.

Soon he found that his creativity increased. He got a deeper understanding of music; spiritual stories began to flow out of his pen.

And gradually he discovered a meaning and security in life that he had never found before.

In 1998, he married. As his wife can testify, he also got married to his computer. He spends several hours a day in front of it, writing spiritual articles, answering email, repairing broken links of his websites and—despite all spiritual growth—getting frustrated when his unruly software doesn't work.

He is deeply into matters of personal growth and inner peace, and he answers questions about them from readers from all over the world. These articles are published on his websites and also sent to the members of his mailing list.

A question Joost Boekhoven often has to answer when abroad, is how to pronounce his surname. He sometimes answers that "Boekhoven" is a combination of "Book" and "Beethoven".

An omen for his life as a musician and an author?

Gem's story is Joost Boekhoven's first spiritual novel.

Gem's Second Book

In *Gem's story* many things of Gem's life have been left untold. There was for instance the mysterious meeting with the baby:

One night we arrived in a village. While we were eating something and talked with the people, we heard a baby crying, all the time. Finally, I asked if I could see the baby. When I got there, the tired-looking mother told me that her boy had been crying literally day and night since his birth, three months ago.

I massaged the tummy of the baby, and his feet, and it didn't help at all. I felt I couldn't reach the boy. He was totally absorbed in some grief. Suddenly, I became aware that my Master entered the hut. For a moment he stood there, silently, a big dark figure in the door opening. Then he knelt down besides the baby, and looked at him with his usual grave expression.

I had seen before how young children reacted to my Master. Often, his strongly built body and wild beard made them afraid. But as soon as my Master bent over the cradle, this baby hiccuped once, as if surprised—and stopped crying.

My Master's expression didn't change. He kept looking at the baby. The boy's face became very peaceful. Then—the baby smiled.

My Master looked at the smile for a moment, slightly frowning. The baby's smile widened, his face bathed in light. His tiny hands reached out to my Master. He poured out his smile to that big person in front of him. I had never seen such openness.

My Master's frown persisted a moment more. Then, all of a sudden, he seemed to let go of something.

He smiled, too.

I discovered later that I had been holding my breath for a long time. The hut and the sounds around me had disappeared; there was only the man and the child. I felt an indescribable link between them.

Finally, my Master stood up again. Without saying anything to me, he left the hut. His smile had faded, but there was an air of lightness around him. I remember he was absorbed in himself, the rest of the night. He didn't speak. But he seemed very open. Relieved, I felt that an old load had fallen off his shoulders.

That day, I just shared my Master's mood and felt happy. I didn't think much about it. Later I sometimes wondered. Who had this baby been before? I'm sure my Master knew the baby, from its previous life.

* * *

This and other mysteries may become part of a second book about Gem's life.

Readers who want to receive news about this novel, can send a mail to secondbook@gemstories. com.

Articles about spirituality

Gem discovered many spiritual truths.

For those who like to know more about them, there is this website:

www.gemstories.com/splash.html

Ask Gem—personal answers to your spiritual questions

It is also possible to get help from Gem herself!

Gem had many years of spiritual experiences and learned to understand human nature very well. She began to help others who had spiritual or psychological questions.

Meet Gem again—read the questions she was asked throughout the years and her answers to them.

- "I can't seem to relax..."-
- "She is so irritating—what shall I do?"

- A depression is your best friend
- "I'm afraid in the dark…"
- How to end a quarrel
- Being here and now
- "How on earth can God be love?"

…and many more.

For those who want to read them, there is **Gem's Mailing list**.

To join the list, send a message to gem@gemstories.com with "mailing list" in the subject line.

Beneath are some of her answers.

Excerpts from Ask Gem—personal answers to your spiritual questions

Hello Gem,

To become a Spiritual Master, should I remain unmarried, like you?

Already Engaged

* * *

Dear Already Engaged,

No. Marriage or celibacy have nothing to do with being a Spiritual Master. A Master is someone who is fully aware of God. He has given up his self-centeredness, his isolation from the universe; he feels the oneness of everything. This is what gives him his happiness and peace of mind.

You can find God inside of yourself and all around yourself, no matter whether you have a family or not. When you feel the desire to be married, then that is your path. When you feel that marriage and attachment would be an obstacle between you and God, you can become a nun or a monk.

Anyone can find God; anyone can experience the oneness of

everything. It will happen when you long for it deeply enough.
Love,
Gem

* * *

Three short questions and answers from Ask Gem

1. Book knowledge
Dear Gem,
I learned meditation from a very good book but I don't feel any more spiritual than before.

You need a very good *teacher*. Books can be good as an introduction or a source of inspiration, but they cannot give you the spiritual energy that you need when you want to start doing meditation. Only a good teacher can do this, and after that, he or she will guide you on your way.
For an article about how to recognize a good teacher, see: http://www.gemstories.com/teachers_b2.html

2. What is Love?
Dear Gem,
Where does love come in?

Yes, without love, you will not be really happy.
But what *is* love?
Is it the feeling you have for your long-time partner? The feeling you have for your latest girlfriend or boyfriend? The feeling you have for your cat, for your work, for strawberry cakes?
Check out Gem's complete answer in the archives of the mailing list.

3. Escapism

Dear Gem,

Isn't spirituality a kind of escape?

Try using it as an escape! You will find that instead, real meditation brings you face to face with yourself. With your good sides and your weak sides. And meditation puts you with both feet on the ground and in the world.

You can resist, of course—most people do for a while. But facing yourself is the best thing you can do in your life. It brings you lasting inner peace, as well as love for others and for yourself.

* * *

Another question from Ask Gem:

Dear Gem,

I am a deep believer in Jesus Christ as our one and only Savior. I have difficulties with things like reincarnation, things that He never talked about.

Do you believe in reincarnation?

Paula

* * *

Dear Paula,

I don't believe in it—I *know* reincarnation exists.

What is a belief? When you like an idea but you can't prove it, you can say, "I believe in this." Belief is something without direct experience. It's just a thought.

It is cold in my room, so I might say to Joost, my editor and biographer, "I believe it's a cold day today."

Joost might answer, "No, the sun is shining, it must be warm outside."

I could answer, "But it's winter, surely it's a cold day."

"No, my almanac here says we will have a *warm* winter."

"Well, I heard the weather forecast for this week and it said there would be snow!"

We could go on like this for a while, quoting our and other people's opinions, and maybe we would get quite hot and bothered because the other didn't share our belief.

The solution, of course, would be to speak from *experience*. In this example, we would only need to go out and feel the temperature for ourselves.

You may think this is a ridiculous example. But in religious and spiritual matters this very thing happens all the time.

People believe very strongly that Jesus is the only one who can bring us to God, or that Muhammad is the only real prophet, or that there is no God at all, or that God exists but that He is an impersonal entity.

Throughout history, Christians have killed Muslims, Muslims have killed Hindus, everybody seems to have killed everybody because they felt that only their belief was right. A belief. Not something backed up by personal experience.

If you ask believers how they know they are right, they will say, "It's in the Bible! It's in the Koran! The Buddha proved it!" And so on.

None of those people will say, "*I* proved it. I meditated for years and expanded my mind beyond all limitations, and then I *experienced* the Truth."

Some may claim that God talked to them directly. If He (It) had really done this, they would have understood that it can't be so that one religion is right and the rest is wrong.

There is not only one path to a mountain top. There are many. Some are easier or faster for certain people, other paths are better for others.

Only watch out for paths that proclaim, "This is the Only Highway To God". They may be dead-end streets.

If a religion or spiritual path gives us a technique to expand our minds—that is most valuable. With a very expanded mind, we can experience the truth for ourselves. We can have direct knowledge.

Paula, thank you for your letter. The fact that you asked the question, gives me the feeling that you are an open-minded person.

I hope you will *experience* knowledge about God and reincarnation.

Love,

Gem

More questions and answers will be posted in the mailing list. For example:

- What kind of meditation is good?
- Should we only listen to spiritual music?
- So when will I finally be feeling spiritual?
- Can vegetarians survive?
- My meditation is very peaceful. But afterwards that feeling quickly disappears.
- My meditation is not at all peaceful. Why?
- They say, "Let God's wish be mine..." But I want to keep my own wishes!
- What will I do in my next life?

To join the list, send a message to gem@gemstories.com with "mailing list" in the subject line.

COSMIC
EGG
BOOKS

If you prefer to spend your nights with Vampires and Werewolves rather than the mundane then we publish the books for you. If your preference is for Dragons and Faeries or Angels and Demons – we should be your first stop. Perhaps your perfect partner has artificial skin or comes from another planet – step right this way. Our curiosity shop contains treasures you will enjoy unearthing. If your passion is Fantasy (including magical realism and spiritual fantasy), Horror or Science Fiction (including Steampunk), Cosmic Egg books will feed your hunger.